A Guardian Unexpected

THE NETTLEBY TRILOGY - BOOK ONE

ROSIE CHAPEL

ULFIRE PTY LTD

First printing of original version 2019
First printing of revised version 2022

ISBN: 978-0-6454794-4-7 (ebook)
ISBN: 978-0-6454794-5-4 (Paperback)

Ulfire Pty. Ltd.
P.O. Box 1481
South Perth
WA 6951
Australia

www.rosiechapel.com

Cover Designed in Canvas by: R Chapel
Images Courtesy Canva and Deposit photos.

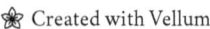 Created with Vellum

Acknowledgments

Thank you to…

Joseph and Eliza Elliott, without whom this story would not exist. I wish I had known them but am proud a little of their blood runs in my veins.

My wonderful Dad for agreeing to let me use his grandparents' story as inspiration for this book, which has become a trilogy.

Mick McGann at British War Graves (www. britishwargraves.co.uk) for kindly sourcing and emailing me a photo of Joseph's headstone and one of Brandhoek Military Cemetery from their incredible site.
The service, he and his team offer, is entirely free and deserving of support.
He has graciously granted me permission to use the image below in this book.

Graham from *A Fading Street Publishing*, for his editing wizardry.

Melanie, for reading a gazillion versions until I'm satisfied.

My long-suffering husband, for putting up with me.

Image Courtesy: British War Graves

In memory of my great grandparents ~
Joseph and Eliza Elliott
~ the inspiration behind this story!

A
Guardian Unexpected

The Nettleby Trilogy - Book One

A WWI Novella

One

July 1915
Nettleby-under-Wold, Lincolnshire
Eliza

S ummer was reaching its height: long sunny days, balmy evenings, and not a rain cloud in sight. Cycling along the narrow road between my home and the village, I stopped pedalling and cruised to a standstill.

Leaning on a hedge, I admired the view; it was one of which I never tired, whatever the season. Even so early in the morning it was already warm, making the landscape shimmer.

In the far distance, the softly undulating wolds unfurled as far as the eye could see, disappearing beyond the horizon. Flowing out to meet them, a patchwork quilt of fields; ripening wheat, barley, and sugar beet, interspersed with potato, cabbage, and onion.

It was a land unchanged for centuries.

The soil — dark, rich, and fertile — provided the perfect conditions for farming and was exploited to its limits. Here and there, I could see people wandering through the fields checking the crops. One or two spotted me and waved, shouting a 'hello' as I picked up speed again. I responded in kind but didn't slow down. I had too much to do today to be dawdling, however beautiful the scenery.

I crunched to a stop outside the only shop in our small village of Nettleby-under-Wold. Propping my bike under the window, I lifted the parcel, lovingly wrapped in brown paper, from the basket between the handlebars.

I hoped Joe would get it in one piece this time. The last one I sent had been opened, probably by the censors. The biscuits I baked especially, mysteriously going astray.

I supposed, I couldn't blame the clerks whose job it was to inspect the mail going to and coming from the men at the front. It must be a godforsaken task, but they weren't the ones in the firing line. They probably went home at night to a decent meal, a warm bed, and dry clothes — or, at the bare minimum, a dry tent where the food was palatable, miles away from the firing line.

Joe, in cleverly couched terms, had made it clear the privations they suffered in the trenches were grim. He *did* mention they were rotated out every eight days or so for a stint in camp, which was something.

His face swam into my mind.

Joseph Elliott was tall and dark-haired, his twinkling green eyes had laugh lines at the corners and, apart from a neatly trimmed moustache, was clean-shaven. We were married not quite three years ago, but I have known him since I was a child. At the grand old age of twenty-seven, he was four years older than me and considered a senior member of his regiment.

He had no need to enlist. His family owned a huge farm and, as the only son, he was entitled to be excused from service, required to work the land, but he wanted to fight for King and Country.

While he had come home for an occasional weekend during the months before he was shipped out to France, no one was going to grant them leave now, and who knew when this senseless war would end?

His letters were brief; they can't tell us too much in case the enemy intercepts the mail, but at least he sends them. They were stored in a box which I kept in the little bedside cabinet.

I tried not to read them too often, the paper had become so thin it would likely fall apart with all the folding and unfolding, but sometimes I needed to see his handwriting. I missed him so much it was an ever-present ache.

Pushing that aside, I opened the door, the jangling bell alerting Maisie Cuthbert to my presence. Maisie was married to Joe's best friend, Fred, and the village shop — which also housed the post office — was the pride and joy of her in-laws.

When Mr Cuthbert was struck down by a nasty bout of pneumonia, Maisie gave up her job selling flowers on the platform at Brigg Station to take over the day-to-day running of the business, until such times as Mr Cuthbert was fit again.

It was supposed to be temporary. She never went back to the flower stall.

Her appearance behind the counter was viewed with pointed brows by the conservative residents of Nettleby...

meaning the majority. This land has been lived on and farmed by the same families since the dark ages, and most hereabouts remained invariably suspicious of newcomers.

While Fred Cuthbert had been born and bred here, his wife hadn't and, to poor Maisie, it must have felt akin to running the gauntlet, facing mistrustful villagers every day. Worse, Maisie still lived in Wrawby... an *indecent* — might as well have been Australia — not quite two miles away... rather than Nettleby, with Fred moving into *her* house after their wedding. In the eyes of the locals, this relegated Maisie to the status of stranger, and it cannot have been easy for her.

Undaunted, Maisie persevered and, refusing to be intimidated, treated everyone to her cheerful smile and friendly chat. Slowly, oh so slowly, they came to accept her and now, a mere seven years later, she was considered one of them.

We have been friends almost since the day we met.

"Parcel for Joe?" she called through, spotting me as I approached the counter.

I nodded. "Yes, hopefully he'll get the whole thing this time. Five pairs of socks, some soap, razors, and enough biscuits to see him through 'til next month." I elaborated, receiving a grin from Maisie as she took it from me to weigh. I was an inveterate knitter and also loved to sew, pastimes I found soothing, plus the soldiers always needed socks.

"I've a few letters here for you. Since you beat old Ken this morning, you might as well take them, and it saves him coming all the way out to the cottage." Maisie handed me a little pile of mail tied with a piece of string.

I flicked through them and felt my heart flutter. A couple of the envelopes looked like they might be from Joe.

"Thank you, Maisie, something to look forward to later." I turned to go. "See you this evening?"

Being a Friday, there was a social on at the village hall. A sing-song, games for the children, and refreshments. It was a pleasant diversion, and an excuse for the women, and the small number of men left in the neighbourhood, to come together and enjoy a good old gossip.

"I'll be there, don't work too hard."

I grinned and waved a goodbye. Dropping the letters into my satchel, I cycled the short distance to the village school. Minutes later, I was absorbed into the activities of the day. It was only a small school, about twenty-five children at full attendance — a rare occurrence.

Nettleby-under-Wold was a rural area, and every family was connected in some way or another to agriculture. Now most of the men had gone off to war, the children had to help where they could. Tending crops was far more important than books and learning.

Two

I didn't get to read my letters until late afternoon. I had less than an hour to sort myself out, before heading back into the village, but I couldn't wait any longer.

Rifling through, I noticed three which looked like they were from Joe. They were always a bit grubby, a good indication they had come from the trenches.

Three! Heavens, it was as though Christmas had come early.

I extracted the top one and slit it open without bothering to look at the front.

It wasn't Joe's handwriting.

It was a short official missive, and the words didn't make sense.

I leant back in the chair and closed my eyes as my whole world went dark.

Oh, please God, no…

Dear Mrs Elliott,
It is with deep regret, I must inform you of the loss of Pte Joseph

Elliott, who is classed as missing presumed dead. On the morning of 4th July, during a vital operation, a section of our battalion was subject to a sustained and heavy bombardment.

When the firing ceased, Pte Elliott along with several of his fellow soldiers, could not be located, and we must assume all were killed during the barrage.

Please accept our sincere condolences for your loss.

There was more, but I didn't read it. It didn't matter anyway, the rest would only be formulaic military speak for any who had lost a loved one. I *did* see it was signed Thad Jenkins, who was Joe's second cousin as well as his commanding officer. Poor bloke, what a wretched task.

Missing presumed dead. How was that possible? The missing bit. Surely someone saw where he fell? My stomach roiled as my brain caught up... it meant whatever happened had obliterated those targeted.

I had just sent him a package; one he would never receive. He would never wear those lovingly knitted socks or eat those ginger biscuits. *Should I be crying?* Probably, but I didn't feel sad, I just felt numb.

I had no idea how long I sat, but when voices broke into my reverie, I glanced out of the window and noticed the light was fading.

"Eliza, are you all right? We missed you at the Hall. Lizzie?" Why are you sitting in the dark?" I heard footsteps as Maisie hurried along the hall and into the room with the third member of our coterie, Polly, on her heels. "Lizzie?" she repeated.

"He's not coming home."

"What on earth are you talking about, me duck? Of course, he's coming home."

"No, he isn't." I thrust the letter under her nose. "He's dead. So dead they can't find him." Anger laced my tones. I bolted out of the chair and began to pace the floor.

Without waiting to be asked, Polly slipped along to the kitchen to put the kettle on. I could hear the rattle of crockery as she bustled about, brewing up the ubiquitous pot of tea.

The only drink which made everything better.

England must be swimming in tea at the moment.

Lighting the lamps, Maisie sat down to read the letter. To her credit, she didn't offer the usual platitudes. She just held my hand until Polly came back with the tea. Pouring three, good strong cups, Polly handed them out and then perched on the window ledge.

"I'm so sorry, Lizzie," Maisie said gently. "Why don't you come home with me tonight? You shouldn't be alone."

"Good idea," Polly agreed, adding something about grieving, and being with other people, and needing time, but I wasn't listening.

Joe was gone. How was I supposed to go on? What was the point?

My mind wandered to the last time I saw him.

It was early August, barely 5 a.m., the sunrise bathing Nettleby in golden pink light.

He looked so smart in his uniform, the badge, denoting he was part of the 5th Battalion Lincolnshire Regiment, gleaming on his cap. His kit, packed as instructed, and his boots polished until he could see his face in them.

He kissed me as though he never wanted it to end but, of course, it had to. He made it to the gate, turned around and came back to kiss me one last time.

"I love you, Lizzie."

"I love you too, Joe. Please come back to me."

"I promise." Too quickly, his loping stride took him down the path and onto the road leading to the village. From there he was heading to Wrawby where he would meet those of his friends who were also leaving that day.

I ran after him a little way.

"Joe," I shouted.

He turned, blew me a kiss, and was gone.

"He promised to come back," I muttered dully.

"He would have done had he any say in the matter," Maisie consoled. "He was determined to come home. He just didn't reckon on the bloody Hun being more determined to prevent him."

"What do I do now?" I heard myself ask, hating that I sounded so pathetic.

"You put one foot in front of the other and keep moving," Polly said, "and never forget we're right behind you, making sure you don't fall."

Two hours later, after persuading Maisie and Polly I was fine on my own and needed to be here surrounded by everything which reminded me of Joe, the house was quiet.

I blew out the lamps and went into the garden, breathing in the light loamy fragrance, which was quintessentially

Lincolnshire. The lonely cry of a curlew drifted on the air — it sounded like a lament.

I stared up at the sky; summer evenings meant daylight lingered until quite late, the colours just beginning to mutate from pinkish grey to inky blue.

Anger consumed me again, and I screamed his name.

"Joe."

Silence, nothing.

Then... *no*... for a split second I was sure I heard my name on the breeze.

Don't be silly, Eliza, you're overwrought and prone to flights of fancy. Sighing, I turned my back on the perfection of the night, locked my door, and trailed upstairs to bed.

Curled up under the covers, endless years of emptiness stretching out before me, I could no longer prevent the memories crowding my head... unsure I wanted to.

My thoughts winged back to the day before my ninth birthday. The day — had either of us know it — when our future was sealed.

Three

September 1900 - Nettleby-under-Wold
Eliza

September was my favourite month. In the main because it was the month of my birthday, but also because there was something special about September.

The days remained warm but without the blazing heat of summer, and the evenings were noticeably cooler, making sleep easier

The fields were being ploughed after the harvest, smoke from an occasional bonfire coiled up into a sky whose dazzling blue had softened to a paler hue, and the air was ever-so slightly hazy. Swallows, gathering for their long flight south, chased down unsuspecting insects.

. . .

I was skipping along the path to Elliotts' farm, on the way to meet my dad, feeling very gown up because Mam had let me come on my own.

"Aye, lass, go on with you." She had smiled when I begged permission. "Just promise me you'll be careful on that track. It's rutted badly after the rains, and you don't need to be taking another tumble." Her wry tone made me blush — my woeful lack of coordination well-known and a source of amusement among my friends.

I spotted a butterfly dancing on the breeze and all other thoughts vanished as I gave chase, running faster and faster along the path, singing a nursery rhyme.

The next moment I was flying. I tried to jerk my body backwards to counter my stumble… Mam's warning ringing in my head… to no avail. I crashed to the ground, knocking the breath from my lungs, and slithered to an ungainly stop.

Winded, I lay motionless attempting to gather my wits and my poise… a futile battle at the best of times.

"Lizzie, Lizzie what did you do this time?" a familiar voice called out as I scrambled to my feet. A loud guffaw followed.

Huffing my vexation, both at my lack of grace and stupid boys, I ignored my rapidly increasing discomfort and, in a valiant attempt to salvage my dignity, stuck my nose in the air and hobbled along the path.

I could see the farm buildings ahead of me… so close. I wanted my daddy, he always made things better. Furiously, I blinked back the tears already dripping down my cheeks. I was nearly nine. I could climb trees, swim in the river, and ride a horse as well as any boy… definitely too old to cry.

"Lizzie." Joe Elliott and Fred Cuthbert skidded to a halt alongside me.

"What?" I sniffed and rubbed the back of my hand across my face.

"Lizzie, you're bleeding." Joe's mirth gentled to genuine concern. He took my arm, led me to the grassy edge of the track, and urged me to sit down. "That was a nasty fall."

"I'm fine," I protested, wriggling out of his grasp, mortified they had seen me trip.

"Of course, you are, but maybe you should sit a minute to catch your breath. Fred." He glanced at his friend who was grinning down at me. "Go fetch Mr Clarke."

"Will do." Fred dashed off towards the farm, while Joe retrieved a relatively clean-looking handkerchief from his pocket and dabbed at my knees.

"Ow," I hissed and tried to dodge the press of the cloth.

"Sit still, goodness, but you are like an eel." Joe chuckled. "Let me wipe off this muck."

I examined my sadly maligned legs and filthy dress. "Mam will tan my hide for this," I groused. "Last thing she said to me when I left the house was 'be careful Lizzie'."

"Tell me what happened?" Joe coaxed, probably more to distract me from what he was doing than in any real interest.

I explained about the butterfly. To his credit, he didn't laugh at me, even though I could tell he thought it hilarious. Joe Elliott was invariably kind. Oh yes, he teased me, and the other girls in the village, remorselessly — as did all the lads, but it was in fun. None of them had a mean bone in their bodies and made sure to watch out for us.

Around Nettleby, everyone knew everyone else. We grew up in and out of each other's homes, usually getting under the feet of whichever mother was baking that day. The older ones kept an eye on the youngsters and, no matter the difference in ages, we all played together. Even pesky nearly-nine-year-olds were not excluded.

Despite the three years separating them, Joe Elliott and Fred Cuthbert had been best friends since the cradle. Lately, I had noticed, we saw less of them. Dad said they were learning to master the different skills required on a busy farm.

The Elliotts, like most in the wolds, had worked this land for generations, the farm passed down from father to son. Fred Cuthbert's family owned the village shop, but Fred was never there; he preferred being outdoors.

"Th-thank you," I stuttered, biting my lip in an effort to staunch the sobs rising in my throat. *I would never live this down. Bad enough Joe and Fred knew, I still had to face Mam.*

"Don't fret, Lizzie." Joe hunkered down next to me and slung a comforting arm around my shoulders. "It's just a few scratches."

"Yes, but Mam warned me to be careful, and look, I've torn my dress. It's all dirty, and it's my birthday tomorrow," I wailed.

Joe ignored that and mopped my tears with the now grubby handkerchief.

He was probably fed up with my whining. *Come on, Lizzie.* I stiffened and tried to shake off his arm.

"I'm fine," I repeated. "I'll wait here for Dad, you can go find Fred," I muttered, grouchily, it must be admitted.

"Hush, I'm not going anywhere 'til your dad gets here. You think I would leave you sitting alone all battered and bruised?" he chided.

"S-sorry, I don't m-mean to be... it's just... and you..." I faltered, not really knowing what I was trying to say.

"Did you bang your head?" He joked and pulled back to study my face.

"Don't be daft." I nudged him with my elbow.

"Hey, watch out, you'll be doing me an injury."

Unconsciously, we fell into the banter typical of our friendship. At the back of my mind, I realised Joe was doing it on purpose, riling me up so I would forget my sore knees and ruined dress.

Dad and Fred appeared, chattering like magpies, their conversation dwindling when they reached us.

Before I could get a word in edgewise, Joe spoke up. "Afternoon, Mr Clarke. Lizzie fell and hurt her knees... and her pride," he added with a straight face.

Dad crouched in front of me and took my hands. "Now, lass, what's all this, and it's your birthday tomorrow." He smiled, the corners of his eyes crinkling.

"I'm sorry, Dad." I gave a resigned shrug. I suspected I was going to spend the rest of the day, and possibly the rest of the week, apologising.

"Naught that can't be mended, love."

"Don't think I want to be nine," I grumbled.

He chuckled. "Ahh, you say that now, but I have it on good authority, you'll change your tune come morning. Want a piggyback?"

"Ohhhh, Dad," I whooped. Piggybacks were a rare treat. I bounded to my feet, wincing when the scratches on my sore knees stretched. "Ouch."

"Up you go." Dad stayed where he was until I had climbed on, then rose slowly, settling me more comfortably.

"Hold on tight," he advised.

"Wait," I pleaded, and twisted to face Joe and Fred. "Thank you. You are both splendid chaps." I beamed at the two lads who flushed and shuffled awkwardly at my effusive and formally delivered gratitude.

I heard Dad stifle a chuckle at their sheepish expressions.

"Don't think on it, Lizzie," Joe mumbled.

"Oh, but I will never forget your gallantry," I assured him. "You were like a knight of the round table, with Fred as your liegeman."

"Come off it." Fred scuffed his shoe in the dirt, and dipped his head.

"Happy Birthday for tomorrow, Lizzie," Joe called as Dad set off home.

I swivelled around again and gave him my best smile.

Joe was all right for a boy.

Four

September 1900 - Nettleby-under-Wold
Joe

Fred and I were heading back to the farmyard when a loud shriek shattered the peaceful afternoon.

We legged it across the field and burst through the gate to see Lizzie Clarke sprawled headlong in the muck.

"Lizzie, Lizzie what did you do this time?" I called out, then muttered to Fred. "By, it's a good job it's not last week. She'd be caked in mud." Several days of rain had turned the fields to swamps and the tracks to rivers. Thankfully, it dried up quickly, but had left the lanes and byways with deep furrows.

Fred barked with laughter. "Rain or shine, Lizzie will allus come a cropper. It's like her head can't keep up with her legs."

"You're not wrong." I chuckled, as I watched Lizzie haul

herself upright. I could see blood oozing from her scuffed knees.

Her face contorted as she, no doubt, made a valiant effort not to cry. Lizzie never cried, she was a stoic little thing, had been since she was old enough to play with the rest of us. Mind, if Lizzie wept every time she took a tumble, she would always be in tears.

She was stomping towards the farm and as we closed the gap. I spotted two fat tears rolling down her dusty cheeks. Something about her dogged stride caused a curious twinge in my chest... which I couldn't fathom and, being a lad of thirteen, ignored.

We reached her side, and my amusement fled at her woebegone expression. "Lizzie…"

"What?" She scrubbed her face, smearing the dirt.

"You're bleeding." I led her to the grassy verge. "Here take a load off and get your breath back."

"I'm f-fine," she hiccupped, and glared at me mutinously.

I agreed with her. No sense in arguing. "Of course, you are, but while you're sitting there, let me clean your knees." I glanced over my shoulder. "Fred, think you can go fetch Mr Clarke?"

"Will do." Fred grinned and galloped off in a cloud of dust.

I dabbed at the blood, not sure whether I was making it better or worse, but at least that and my questions distracted Lizzie, who told me she had been chasing a butterfly.

I swallowed the mirth bubbling up inside me. Lizzie did not look disposed to be amused. Instead, I concentrated on cleaning as much of the grit and mud out of the scratches as possible.

She stuttered a thank you, and I mopped up her tears, without comment, then kept her chatting until Fred returned, Mr Clarke in tow.

Relieved I could hand Lizzie over to her father, I was left speechless when she called us splendid chaps, adding that I was like a gallant knight. Fred wasn't particularly chuffed at being referred to as my liegeman, especially given he was three years my senior.

As Mr Clarke piggybacked Lizzie home, I wished her a happy birthday for the next day.

Her sunny smile all but split her face.

She wasn't bad for a girl, wasn't Lizzie.

September 1906 - Nettleby-under-Wold
Joe

Bouquet of flowers in hand, I rapped on the door of number five Rothwell Lane. There was no sound from within and, for one awful moment, I thought nobody was home, then Mr Clarke was there ushering me inside.

"In you come, Joseph, take a seat." Mr Clarke never shortened anyone's name. "Eliza will be down shortly... I hope. Heavens, what a going on. You know how girls are. The shoes *must* match the dress, the dress *has to* be just right. I didn't think our lass had that many." He chuckled with the tolerance of a father who thought the fuss was nonsense but loved his daughter all the more for it.

"Thank you, sir." I sank into the nearest chair and tried to think of something intelligent to say, while surreptitiously rubbing my palms along my trousers. Lizzie had agreed to go with me to a dance at the church hall, and I was beset by nerves. I had never asked a girl anywhere before, let alone somewhere as important as the Harvest Dance.

"Stop fretting, son," Mr Clarke said after I started to speak three times only to stop for fear of sounding like a gibbering idiot.

"Sorry, sir, it's just... I..." *Joe get it together*, I admonished inwardly, and drew a calming breath. "I don't want to let Eliza, or you, down." I blurted out, flushing bright red.

Mr Clarke shook his head good-humouredly at my discomfiture. "All you have to do is behave like the gentleman I know you have grown up to be, and everything else will be fine."

He asked me an innocuous question about my day, which led to an interesting discussion about farming techniques, until I heard the thud of feet on the stairs. I stood up and straightened my jacket.

Lizzie came into the room.

Her dress, the colour of lilacs, fell to just above her ankles and floated around her as she came towards me. Her glossy dark hair was piled up in a mass of curls caught neatly in a headband the same shade as her dress. She looked a trifle uncomfortable, which steadied my own vague sense of panic.

I suspected my eyes were on stalks. Lizzie... no, tonight she was Eliza... looked so beautiful, and it was hard to believe she was only fifteen. *How had I missed her transformation from tomboy to elegant young lady?* I swallowed an anxious gulp.

"Good evening, Eliza." I made a creditable effort *not* to sound like a half-wit and bowed slightly — a gesture that seemed entirely natural under the circumstances.

Lizzie gaped at my use of her full name. I think it was probably the first time I had addressed her thus. Clearly, this was going to be an evening of firsts. I felt the heat wash up my face again and cursed my lack of gentility. I was just a farmer's lad, what right did I have to escort so chic a young lady to a dance?

Her eyes narrowed, suspiciously. "Are you making fun of me?"

"N-No, I never... I would n—"

"Are you sure?" Hands on hips, she interrupted my stammered denial.

"Lizzie," Mrs Clarke, who had entered the parlour behind her daughter, remonstrated gently. "Joe is being polite. Something you could learn to be."

"Sorry, Mam. Sorry, Joe." Lizzie smiled shyly. "You look very smart." Her grey eyes held mine, and I wanted to lose myself in their smoky depths. "Shall we go?"

"Yes, no wait... these are for you." I had almost forgotten, and handed her the bouquet, which I had been hiding behind my back.

"Joe..." she gasped, lifting the blooms to her nose to inhale their delicate scent. "...these are glorious. What a lovely surprise. Thank you."

"My pleasure," I said gruffly.

"How about I put these in water for you?" Lizzie's Mam intervened, taking the flowers, and handing her daughter a shawl. "Just in case it gets chilly later," she added and kissed Lizzie's cheek. "We'll be there shortly."

With the sensitivity of parents who recognised the awkwardness of youth, Mr and Mrs Clarke ushered us into the hall and returned to the parlour.

I opened the front door and paused, crooking my arm invitingly.

To my everlasting relief, Lizzie accepted, her hand sliding around my elbow and coming to rest on my sleeve.

We stepped into the early autumn evening. The sun had just dipped below the horizon. The sky above our heads ablaze with streaks of fire mixed with purple and pink.

"Oh, what a marvellous sunset," Lizzie exclaimed and turned to face me.

Her delighted smile reminded me of the day she had tumbled after chasing a butterfly… and just like that, I understood the elusive emotion which had teased my senses ever since.

I was in love with Eliza Clarke.

Five

September 1906 - Nettleby-under-Wold
Eliza

My first dance. I wanted to remember every minute of it... the more so because I was there with Joe. I couldn't believe it when he invited me to go with him. *Me...* Lizzie Clarke.

At, nineteen, Joe worked full-time for his father on the farm. Had done for years. I was keenly aware... I might only be fifteen, but I had eyes... he had gone from callow youth to handsome young man. He had shot up, and was easily a good head taller than me, with muscles you could count... not that I did.

I had heard the older girls talking about him. They considered him quite the catch, yet, as far as I could tell, he didn't seem bothered. He continued to be his usual genial self, never giving the impression he was interested in anything more serious.

Until recently.

During the past year or so, I had bumped into him at the school gates with increasing frequency.

Initially, I assumed it to be a coincidence. He knew plenty of people in the village and passing the school at day's end would not be unexpected, especially as some of his mates, hoping to get into university were still pupils. Joe was the sort of lad who wouldn't think twice about waiting for a friend.

Of late, I had cause to revise my assumption. It appeared the reason he turned up like clockwork when the bell rang… was me.

The afternoon when first he asked whether he might walk me home, made me giggle because it sounded so grown up. Almost without me noticing, it became a regular thing — as flattering as it was unsettling.

If I had homework, he carried it. His behaviour was reminiscent of characters in my story books. Courteous and considerate, the consummate gentleman, in fact. Never overstepping the boundaries of expected etiquette.

I treasured that time, just the two of us, but kept it to myself; I hadn't even told Mam. He was nineteen, and I *did* wonder… out of all the girls in the neighbourhood who were closer to his age, much more sophisticated and far prettier… why me?

Now, I was accompanying him to the Harvest Dance. In my head it was a tacit declaration of intent. As village events go, this was second only in prestige to Midnight Mass at Christmas although, obviously, much less restrained.

A gentleman did not escort a lady to this particular dance unless he was attracted to her… romantically.

Did I *want* Joe to find me attractive?

I most certainly did…

…but I was only fifteen.

Doubtless, he was just being kind. Joe probably saw me as nothing more than the kid who wheedled her way into their games, more like a sister — studiously ignoring the dull ache my conjecture engendered.

The village hall had been decorated within an inch of its life. Paper chains were strung above our heads. Arranged in a loose circle around the dance floor, several tables covered in gaily coloured gingham. Each sported a candle, and a centre-piece made of plaited straw tied with bright ribbon. Assorted lamps and candelabra bathed the hall in a welcoming glow.

Here and there, huge displays of harvest fruits and vegetables, reminiscent of the village fete, added to the autumnal ambience. A veritable feast was laid out on the counter in the kitchen, the hatch folded back, allowing people to queue at both sides.

A band played in one corner and couples were already dancing.

"Oh, Joe, this is so exciting." I squeezed his arm, and tried not to squeal my exhilaration, but I'm sure my voice rose several notches.

He grinned. "Let's find a table, then I'll fetch us some food."

We greeted people on our way through the throng, and chose to sit at the opposite side of the dance floor to the band. That way, we could talk without shouting. Joe took my shawl and folded it over the back of my chair then disappeared into the melee in search of sustenance.

I patted my hair to make sure it hadn't escaped its confines and settled back to enjoy the happy scene.

Joe was gratifyingly attentive. We danced and chatted, nibbled on far too many tasty morsels, drank fruit punch, and danced some more.

Our respective parents played chaperone for a while before joining their own friends, and leaving us to our own devices, although, periodically, I felt Mam's eyes on me.

My concern, we might run out of things to talk about proved unfounded. Our conversation flowed as smoothly as the couples twirling around the floor.

The whole evening was magical.

"Lizzie."

It was close to midnight when the curious note in Joe's tone had me twisting to face him. "Something wrong?" I was only half concentrating, absorbed by the entertainment.

"No, everything is the rightest it has ever been," he replied, less than coherently.

I spluttered with mirth. "The rightest?"

He grimaced, and rubbed one hand around his nape. "Sorry, I am not very good at this."

"At what?" Intrigued, I gave him my full attention.

He stared at me, his jaw working. For no apparent reason, I held my breath.

He started to speak, stopped, then started again.

"Lizzie, how would you feel about being my girl?" His question came out in a rush.

Startled, this was the *last* thing I expected him to say, I searched his face. *Was he pulling my leg?* His demeanour was grave, and his eyes wary. Joe was nervous. I could not recall ever seeing Joe Elliott nervous.

Something told me this moment would stay with me for the rest of my life.

I exhaled on a barely suppressed whoosh.

"Y-your girl...?" My heart did a somersault and I felt a smile as wide as the wolds beginning to form but managed to school my features... *behave like an adult, Lizzie, not a giddy child.*

"My girl... that is if you want... and your parents approve and..." he trailed off, and raked his fingers through his hair, but didn't drop his gaze.

I was tongue-tied.

Another first.

Greatly daring, he took my hand, his thumb stroking over my knuckles.

"Lizzie, you captured my heart before I knew what love was. I feel as though you are the other half of me, and that without you, I will wither away." His cheeks flared bright red. "I don't suppose you are even thinking about love or courtship, and I have little to offer someone who shines as brightly as you, but I promise to love you throughout this life and into the next."

I was dreaming. I *had* to be dreaming. Men didn't talk like that anymore. Joe's words evoked fairy tales or folklore — damsels, knights, and chivalry. I looked down at our hands. His fingers had come to rest on my palm. The sensation, utterly delectable.

I was only fifteen. What did I know about love?

I studied him — his guarded expression and his beautiful green eyes, which normally twinkled but, right now, were serious.

What if someone else won his affection? I asked myself, to be startled by an inexplicable melancholy.

A curious notion tickled my subconscious... doubtless triggered by my love of heroic tales... but it refused to be doused. *Was this our destiny? A bond preordained by Fate, quiescent until the opportune moment.*

Yes, my sentiment was fanciful, but an emotion I had never experienced suffused me. Later, when I reviewed the evening, in meticulous detail, I swore it was because my soul recognised its mate.

"Joe..." I husked.

His face crumpled, and his gaze dropped. He expected me to reject his advance.

Without thinking, I interlaced our fingers. "Joe," I repeated quietly.

His eyes slid back to mine.

"I would be honoured."

Six

August 1914 - Nettleby-under-Wold
Eliza

How had we gone from peace to war in a heartbeat? Worse, why did our lads think they ought to be involved? We would do well to keep out of it. It wasn't our fight.

Except, obviously, it was.

To allow one country to ride roughshod over another was unacceptable. If the rest of the world stood aside and permitted such atrocities, who was next, and where would it stop?

I knew the reasoning behind it. In the simplest terms, Gavrilo Princip, a Bosnian Serb, assassinated the Austro-Hungarian Archduke, Franz Ferdinand.

A heinous act but one which, had wiser heads prevailed, should have been contained *before* it escalated beyond sense.

Efforts to resolve the problem by diplomatic means,

failed. Austria-Hungary declared war on Serbia, and a convoluted system of alliances drew half of Europe into the conflict.

While cognisant the situation was a good deal more complex, I reckoned that covered the basic cause.

Joe, already a member of the Lincolnshire Territorial Force, had been, with most of the neighbourhood lads, at the brigade's annual camp when war was declared.

The announcement changed everything and, instead of playing soldier, they were catapulted into the real thing, dispatched to Grimsby for home defence and where they would also be billeted.

Neither of us had any idea what the coming months held; it was sobering.

We had been married only a couple of years, delaying our wedding so I could fulfil my dream of being a teacher. Now, I wished I had not been so selfish. We could have had more time together.

Attired in his new uniform, Joe took my breath away. How was it that an outfit worn to distinguish killers from inno-cents... for, fundamentally, they *were* killers, however justifi-ably... turned even the most average-looking chap into a devastatingly handsome hero.

Of course, my Joe was already devastatingly handsome, the uniform merely enhanced his good looks. No wonder women swooned over military men.

"I don't want you to go," I whispered for the umpteenth

time as he held me close and kissed me with an almost desperate ardour.

"I do not want to leave you, love, but to stand by and do nothing, while my friends face this travesty would be cowardly. I'm only going as far as Grimsby and they say it'll be over by Christmas."

"Do you truly believe either of those things?" I countered.

He shrugged into the pattern webbing, then hefted his neatly packed haversack onto his shoulder. "I have faith, wisdom will prevail."

I envied his optimism.

"The farm…" I knew this last-ditch attempt to guilt him into staying was a waste of breath, but the words spilled out anyway.

"Pa has it covered." He leant back to study me, tucking a lock of hair behind my ear. "I must do this, Lizzie."

"I know." I choked on a sob.

The clock on the mantle chimed five.

"It's time."

I swallowed my dread and my tears, brushed my hands down the front of his jacket smoothing non-existent wrinkles, and opened the door.

Fragrant summer air rushed in to greet us. The sun peeking above the horizon painted the clear sky in shades of pink and gold.

The perfection of that morning remained indelibly imprinted in my mind.

Murmured endearments were not enough. They would never be enough, and the fear this was the last time I would see him sent ice slithering down my spine. I summoned up a genuine smile, adamant Joe would not see me weep.

He was correct, he was only going to Grimsby, a short train ride away. The lurking dread this was only the first step on a much longer journey gnawed at me, but I forced it aside.

"I love you, Lizzie."

"I love you too, Joe. Please come back to me." I hugged him and our lips met in a fierce caress.

"I promise."

He was meeting Thad Jenkins in the village, the pair heading to Wrawby where Fred would join them. He had taken less than ten strides along the road, when I ran to the gate.

"Joe," I shouted.

He turned, blew me a kiss, and was gone.

I watched until he disappeared from view.

What did I do now? At a loss, I sank onto the front step, trying to plan my day, my life. "Come on Lizzie," I chivvied myself. "Don't be so dramatic. Joe goes out from dawn 'til dusk most days anyway. You have plenty to do."

Only I didn't. I realised my days revolved around Joe's schedule. Up with the lark to make his breakfast and pack his lunch. Once he left for the farm, I tidied the house and — depending on the day — popped down to the shop, did the washing, baked, ironed, changed the bed, and assisted at the school.

Assisted at the school... a seemingly benign phrase but, bearing in mind the alternative, somewhat momentous.

It was customary for women to give up their careers when they married, and turn their skills to being housewives. Thankfully, especially for me, during the last decade or so, the status quo had been redefined.

Several of my friends had continued to work in their chosen profession, long after wedding vows had been uttered, and I too balked at the constraints. Easier said than done... the situation required delicate handling.

Then, I had a brain wave. To implement an idea which had fascinated me when I was training. One whereby, I could utilise my hard-earned qualifications, and ought not ruffle too many feathers.

My proposal, while greeted with scepticism on some fronts, also solved an acute problem.

With Joe's support and the endorsement of the school board... on which, fortuitously, both our fathers sat... I was approved to be a special needs tutor, catering to those children who struggled to keep up with their peers.

Unusual? Undeniably, but the school did not have the resources to hire another member of staff for a handful of hours a week. That I had volunteered my time swayed their vote and, if nothing else, my training wasn't going to waste.

I loved it. My small group of children, while challenging, were a joy to teach, soaking up information like sponges. Their enthusiasm and progress extinguished the lingering doubts of a cynical few as to the wisdom of the project.

Sitting with my head against the door jamb, it occurred to me that if this war dragged on, I might be asked to resume my role as a full-time teacher. Not the way I wanted my wishes to be granted.

I blew a weighty sigh and pushed myself upright. The trick was to stay busy. Perhaps, that way, I wouldn't notice Joe's absence quite as much.

Thank goodness for Maisie and Polly, I could not ask for better friends.

Polly, I have known for ever. My age, she hopes to become a nurse and has already applied to the nursing schools in Nottingham. Maisie, I had met just before she married Fred — Joe's best friend. We hit it off immediately and have been closer than sisters ever since.

In some respects, we were kindred spirits.

Maisie had dreamt of buying the flower stall where she used to work, but ended up running the shop in Nettleby, after Fred's dad took ill. I had dreamt of being a teacher, and achieved my goal, only to give it up when I married Joe.

Fortuitously, Maisie discovered she loved working at the shop... especially the post office side of the business, and I had wangled my part-time role at the school.

I liked to think it was simply our respective dreams evolving to suit our lives, which I doubt either of us would change given the choice.

Grinning at my philosophical turn of thought, I took one last look along the empty road, and began the rest of my day.

$\mathcal{S}$even

March 1915 - Le Havre
Joe

A call went up…
  "France. I can see France." It rippled along the ranks of men and, through the drizzle which had hounded us since Southampton, a coastline loomed. We jockeyed for a good position at the rails, the better to see foreign soil.

Among my comrades, the only person to have ventured beyond English shores was Thad Jenkins, our Warrant Officer — who also happened to be my second cousin. He spent two weeks in France on his honeymoon, an unheard of extravagance — sadly, his wife had died a couple of years back.

I bet he never thought he'd be returning under these circumstances or be grateful for being widowed. I was blessed to be married to Lizzie, but hated being a cause of worry.

. . .

The awed exclamations suggested, for the majority, this was a first.

That we were following in the footsteps of countless other soldiers who had arrived here during the past few months was bittersweet. The oft-repeated catch cry, 'It'll be over by Christmas,' had dwindled quickly, as hope for a swift cessation in hostilities was dashed.

My Pa had been in the Boer War, as had Lizzie's. Weapons had become more efficient and infinitely more deadly since then, and he did *not* want me coming over here. Given the Elliotts were a farming family, I was entitled to an exemption from service, but I refused to be talked out of it.

Like I had said to Lizzie all those months ago, to remain behind while my friends faced this abomination would be cowardly in the extreme. If I died protecting all I held dear, then at least I would meet my maker with a clear conscience.

As I watched the port come into view, my thoughts strayed.

The days after saying goodbye to Lizzie were chaotic. Stationed at Grimsby to guard the docks and the harbour, we had scarcely settled into our billets when we were shunted off to Belper in Derbyshire. This stunningly beautiful area of England seemed an odd centre for military activities.

That said, you could not fault the welcome of the locals. They were marvellous and made us feel right at home. Thad was so impressed, he wrote to the local paper, thanking the townsfolk for their goodwill to a motley bunch of strangers.

In that idyllic backwater, the Lincolnshires were asked to volunteer for active duty overseas.

The response was mixed. The time of year meant the regiment was already well below capacity. Crops don't harvest themselves and, given no one was prepared to let produce go to waste for want of a couple of months, there was visible reluctance among men torn between protecting the country and feeding the country.

A compromise was reached. Those deemed indispensable to their local agricultural industry returned home. The rest of us travelled south to Luton where our training began in earnest.

As the year ticked by, the number of volunteers and new recruits increased until we hit full strength. Leave was a rare luxury and, in my humble opinion, granted more to boost morale than for any other reason. I savoured the days I spent with Lizzie, keenly aware they could be my last.

All that training was about to be put to the test.

I was interested to note, despite hearing more French than English, Le Havre was no different from any other port — large, noisy, and dirty. After disembarking, we had a brief hiatus in a rest camp before boarding a train which would take us to the front.

The front, people bandied that term about as though it was some splendid town where visitors could take the waters or explore stately homes and their perfectly manicured gardens. A place where the wealthy holidayed, not a line of fortified trenches stretching from the English Channel to the Swiss border, which had become, in essence, one long graveyard.

A place where we too might be laid to rest.

I shook off despondent thoughts and concentrated on the scenery. It was about 175 miles to Arras, through beautiful rolling countryside, the landscape of which was familiar — mainly agricultural. Before nostalgia got a foothold, I turned my attention to the conversation swirling around me, relegating Nettleby to the periphery of my mind... for a little while.

April 1915 - Flanders
Joe

Despite sitting through numerous lectures relating to life at the front, none of us was prepared for the reality. A holiday it most definitely was not, and brought into sharp focus the persistence, from certain quarters, to glorify war, as though by doing so the conflict became less... fatal.

It reminded me of a history lesson at school. The teacher had explained it was not uncommon during past conflicts for well-to-do gentlemen to take their families to safe vantage points in order to observe a battle through viewing glasses — much like they were attending an opera. The 'spectators' were provided with a blow-by-blow account of the confrontation by a military liaison, and often made a day of it.

While that had sounded like a bit of an adventure to a child in a classroom, seeing it first-hand, begged the question why anyone would choose to *watch* people fight to the death. The philosophical part of me argued — reasonably, to my chagrin — that it should come as no surprise, it had been going on in one form or another since the world began.

Neither was there time to reflect on such lunacy; from

the moment we arrived at Ploegsteert we were kept busy from dawn 'til dusk... probably no bad thing.

If I thought life as a farmer had prepared me for strenuous activity, I was sorely mistaken. The effort required to dig trenches in wet, sludgy soil, day in and day out, was backbreaking. Worse, this was all undertaken while dodging random volleys of bullets.

To be honest, the weeks blurred into one, as did the battles.

From the beginning of April when we went into the line opposite Spanbroekmolen, a German fortification on the Messines Ridge, I lost count of the names of various villages, ridges, and hills.

I followed orders, kept my head low, and prayed we would survive the day.

The nightmare assumed epic proportions.

Not satisfied with traditional weapons, the bloody Hun revealed the depths to which they would sink by unleashing a thick yellow gas against the allied troops. The suffocating cloud resulted in untold casualties and thousands of deaths, and allowed the Germans to advance unopposed, taking prisoners and guns.

Reports filtering back were gruesome in their content, and we praised the good Lord our position meant, thus far, we had escaped so horrendous a fate.

Not that the enemy neglected our division, they just subjected us to another form of torture... bombarding us with mortar fire instead of gas, detonating mines under our trenches.

Oddly, this strengthened rather than weakened our resolve.

No way in hell were we going to let the buggers win.

June 1915 - Flanders
Joe

"If this weather doesn't pick up, we'll be buried alive by these damn trenches, and the Germans will take the line without needing to fire a shot. What I would do for a bath," Fred grumbled one miserable morning in June.

I glanced up and sniggered. He was dripping in mud. "You're supposed to dig the hole, not wallow in it."

"You're a fine one to talk." He nodded at my uniform which was equally splattered.

"Nowt we can do," Charlie Townsend, one of my mates from Wrawby, interjected. "This stuff is like bloody glue. Good job we're on rotation tomorrow, if my clothes dry out, I'll never get 'em off." He gave a resigned shake of his head.

"Good camouflage though." I parried. "Maybe we should employ it as a tactic. Coat ourselves in mud, then shimmy across no man's land on our bellies. The Hun'd probably think it was just the ground settling after one of their artillery attacks, and we'd overrun them before they realised what was happening."

"More like they'd strafe the lot of us because we look like a horde of giant worms. Joseph Elliott, use your noggin." Fred pulled a comical grimace while Charlie, and Harry Alderton, another Nettleby lad, chuckled.

"No sense of adventure," I retorted.

We bantered back and forth. The ludicrous conversation lightened the gloomy mood, and by nightfall the rain had stopped.

The next day we headed back to camp and a brief respite.

Eight

June 1915 - Flanders - Rest Camp
Joe

Clad in clean, dry uniforms, and with full stomachs, Fred and I sat outside the tent we shared with four other blokes, to write to our wives.

I strove to make my news cheerful, avoiding any mention of the war — it would be struck out anyway — and thanked her for the parcel, I was handed when I arrived in camp the previous night. Her neatly sewn handkerchiefs and carefully knitted pairs of socks had made it past the censors — her biscuits had not, which irked me. Greedy wretches. Couldn't they allow us an odd treat?

Our letters finished, Fred and I chatted over a piping hot cup of tea. I slouched in the chair, stretched out my legs, and let the warmth of the summer evening wash over me.

"Not a bad place for a break," I quipped.

"Better than that place over yonder." Fred jerked his head

in the direction of the front. "The other guests are way too noisy."

We both laughed.

Something I didn't think possible in this theatre of bloodshed.

I feared I was growing immune to the destruction being wrought. Grisly remains no longer made me wretch. I didn't duck when I heard the whine of an incoming shell, or flinch at the sound of an explosion.

The discordant symphony of war had become less disturbing than the dawn chorus in Nettleby.

June 1915 - Nettleby-under-Wold
Eliza

I heard the chime of a bell and stuck my head out of the window to see a tow-headed youth brandishing a brown envelope. My lips twitched at his antics at the same time as a thrill ran through me. *A letter from Joe...?*

"Mail, Mrs Elliott," Davy Ledwell bawled, adding, as though he had read my thoughts, "I reckon it's from your Joe."

"Coming." I all but galloped down the stairs and burst through the front door, skidding to an inelegant halt at the gate.

Davy handed over the letter, with a cheeky grin.

I responded in kind, asking after his grandpa.

Ken Ledwell was a fixture in Nettleby and had been our Postie for decades. A month ago, he'd come off his bike and sprained his ankle, prompting young Davy to take over his round.

I'm sure the extra pocket money was the prime motivator rather than any sense of responsibility to his grandfather but, give him his due, he had stuck to it, even on wet days.

"He'll be back next week. Doc says he's right as rain."

"What will you do with the spare time?"

"Sleep." He pulled a droll face. "Gotta go, see you at school." He peddled off at high speed, singing at the top of his voice, blithely oblivious of the early hour.

Shaking my head, I retraced my steps, trying to decide whether to read the letter now or keep it until I got home.

I couldn't wait.

Carefully, I opened the envelope, and unfolded the flimsy sheet.

Just seeing Joe's scrawl warmed me. It was like a tiny piece of him in my hands.

I glanced at the clock on the mantle. I had half an hour before I needed to be on my way. Plenty of time to savour his news.

June 20th, 1915

That was only four days ago.

The speed with which mail reached us from the front was incredible.

My darling Lizzie,

I hope this finds you well. Thank you for your letter with accompanying extras.

I wish I could say we all enjoyed your biscuits but some selfish ~~sod~~ soul between there and here purloined them. I'm not pointing fingers, but I reckon you can guess.

It would be satisfying to think the buggers choked on the crumbs, but your baking is much too delicious for that to happen.

I chuckled, despite being aggrieved at the behaviour of the censors who I had no doubt were responsible for the missing biscuits.

Life here continues at its usual pace. Tedium interspersed with chaos. I have no desire to upset you by describing my routine, suffice it to say we continue to look out for each other.

As the weather is the least offensive topic of conversation, I must tell you, we have been plagued with incessant rain for days. I know that snippet will thrill you all the way to your toes.

My chuckle morphed into a mischievous giggle. It was a standing joke that, at social gatherings, no one ever talked about anything of importance, stubbornly sticking to the vagaries of the British weather.

A topic honed over years of use, it could be stretched out for hours, and had become an endless source of hilarity. With wicked glee, we tried to provoke people by introducing a wholly different subject, preferably controversial, just to see how fast they steered it back to the weather.

We had even timed it. The longest deviation was seven minutes.

Shaking my head in reminiscence, I continued reading.

The lads and I resembled mud monsters when we came off the line, and the queue for a bath stretched right around the camp. At the end of it all, we finished up with clean, dry uniforms, and a decent meal. I feel almost human again.

Thad has organised a football match for this afternoon, that ought to banish the fidgets and give us a good stretch of the legs and lungs.

You'd like _____, Lizzie.

I squinted at the space where a word had been scrubbed out, then checked the reverse of the sheet, in hopes of deciphering something — to no avail. Clearly, the censors preferred I, or anyone else who might intercept this letter, did not know where my husband was based.

They had erased it very thoroughly. Even the following lines offered no hint... presumably, the censors deemed *their* removal unnecessary.

The countryside is beautiful, and not dissimilar to the wolds. Softly undulating landscape, lush farmland with small villages scattered about. So many birds, their melody in stark contrast with the rattle of guns and boom of shells. Maybe after this is over, we might consider a holiday here.

The nights are the best, especially once the guns fall silent. Night after night, at least until this blasted rain — there I go talking about the weather again... tut tut — the sky is crystal clear and laden with stars.

Watching the moonrise is when I feel closest to you. It reminds me of all those evenings we sat on the front step and did the same.

Unexpected tears blurred the words at Joe's poetic turn of phrase. Heavens, he knew how to tug on a girl's heartstrings. Memories of those evenings reared up in my mind.

We had developed a habit of having supper outside, picnic style. Nothing fancy, a pot of tea and couple of slices of cake or sometimes a sandwich. Sitting on the step, we waited for the moon to begin its time honoured journey, watching vivid sunsets fade to pink twilight, vying to be the first to spot the Evening Star.

It was a tranquil pastime, we rarely talked, relishing the quiet and, during the summer months, it was often well after midnight before we got to bed. Perhaps a trifle rash, given Joe was usually gone by six, but I was glad we had ignored common sense — I would not trade those precious hours together for all the tea in China.

I was *not* going to cry. I blinked away the suspicion of dampness to read the rest of Joe's letter. He signed it with all his love, and I pressed my lips to his name. "Come home to me, Joe," I murmured to the empty room.

The cheerful chime of the clock striking seven penetrated my reverie. I needed to get a move on. Sliding the sheet back into its envelope, I hurried upstairs to add it to the other letters Joe had sent. I stroked my fingers over the meagre collection, my only link to my husband.

Before the familiar ache of separation crept in, I dropped them into the box. Closing the lid, I tucked it neatly into the bedside cabinet, and turned my attention to the day ahead.

My half-formed prediction had come to fruition. The school board had offered to reinstate me to fill the breach left by those who had volunteered for service. Teaching and lesson preparation left little time to wallow — a selfish indulgence, bearing in mind how many families had a loved one at the front.

Neither had we eluded the wrath of war. Ships transporting casualties and coffins berthed with distressing frequency. To date, Nettleby had escaped the latter, but we knew of men in the vicinity, sent home suffering from shrapnel wounds.

It was only a matter of time before death came to our doorstep.

Nine

July 1915 - Western Front, Flanders
Joe

"We can't hold out much longer," Thad Jenkins announced during a lull in the shelling. "The trenches are on the verge of collapse and won't last if this keeps up. Our priority now is to withdraw to the support line then get the injured to the field hospital before we end up entombed in ten feet of mud."

We stared at our Warrant Office in consternation. This was no easy feat. We had been under constant fire for days, resulting in several casualties, who we couldn't transfer out because, every time we tried to move, the enemy launched another barrage.

Darkness brought no relief; the bastards were committed to annihilating every last one of us — making us equally committed not to grant them any such satisfaction.

A laudable conviction, but one which did not solve our current predicament.

We knew the trenches had been weakened — we had been shoring them up with duckboards and whatever else we could find in hopes, once the rain stopped, the walls would dry out before they completely disintegrated. Even while Thad was speaking, the sides were crumbling, clumps of mud splashing into the puddles at our feet.

"What we need is the sun to come out," a young private, Jack Phillips, groused. "This is supposed to be France in the summer, not bloody Cleethorpes in the winter. I came here to get a tan, and I've ended up with webbed feet."

His attempt at humour, raised a half-hearted laugh.

The weather had been execrable. Following a lengthy spell of warm sunny days, the rain had returned in earnest, undoing all our efforts to stabilise the trench network.

"What we need is a diversion," Fred mused, almost to himself.

"Don't mumble, Corp'ral." Thad gave Fred his undivided attention. "Care to repeat that?"

"We need something to divert their attention long enough to evacuate the system. Doesn't need to be too complicated, I reckon we only need an hour, two at most."

Ideas from the sublime to the ridiculous were tossed out, until Thad put up his hand for quiet.

"Oi, keep your voices down, you're like a flock of geese. I prefer not to be blown out of my boots *before* we have a chance to withdraw. I think that last suggestion could be the winner." He stalled what was becoming a heated debate and arched a long-suffering brow.

"Perhaps winner is the wrong choice of words, how about

the least appalling option? It's a good job none of you oversee strategy, the Germans would be marching along Oxford Street already." He didn't grin as much as he looked less harried.

"Right, to make this work we need the Hun to believe the attack is genuine, not a ruse. That entails a lot of noise and a lot of gunfire." Thad ran his mind over the trench network, and indicated a point beyond our sight were it zigzagged rather wildly.

"If we launch it from the far end of that trench, we have a fighting chance. Ten ought to suffice." He surveyed the motley bunch of men hunched against the drizzle, all of whom he knew.

I watched Thad's expression harden. To select who would live and who would probably die was brutal. I didn't want my cousin, who was also my friend, to shoulder that burden alone. I wasn't stupid, the prospect of survival was minimal at best.

I lifted my hand. "I'm up for it," I offered quietly.

"Joe," Fred hissed. "Bloody hell, man, do I have to shoot you? I cannot tell Lizzie you volunteered for this mission. She will kill me."

"Hopefully, you won't have to but, if the few save the many, I can live, fingers crossed, with that."

"I'm not letting you go without me. If I do, *Maisie* will kill *me*," Fred muttered and started to raise his hand.

Thad cut across him. "No, Corporal, I need you in charge of the withdrawal."

The abject relief on Fred's face was comical.

I nudged his shoulder. "Watch those buggers." I inclined my head towards the German line. "You know how swiftly they take down the unwary."

"I'll be careful," he promised.

Others were quick to follow my lead, and we had double the requisite number in a matter of seconds. Aware it could get out of hand, resulting in more men creating the diversion than helping evacuate the trenches, Thad picked the first nine who had volunteered after me.

He dispatched the rest to prepare for the exodus, while he outlined the plan twice more. "You all clear?" He looked each one of us in the eye and, at our nod, shook hands. "May God protect you," he murmured and spun on his heel, only to turn back and grasp me by the shoulders.

"I don't have to remind you what Aunt Ada's going to say about this, so you'd better not cark it." He fixed me with his serious gaze, and I felt his great paw tighten in a squeeze. "Thank you, Joe, you're a bloody inspiration."

Startled, I tried to splutter a denial but, in the seconds it took for my brain to form a coherent rebuttal, Thad was out of hearing range.

There was little time to ponder the insanity of our tactics... no bad thing. I did manage a hasty goodbye to Fred, Charlie, and Harry.

"Don't you dare die," Fred growled and, to my surprise, drew me into a brotherly hug.

"Tell Lizzie..." I started.

"No, dammit, you'll tell her yourself," he interrupted gruffly. As the four of us stared at each other, a single ray of sunshine cleaved the grey cloud, bathing our huddled quartet in its beam.

A good omen?

I prayed it was so.

"Nice day for it." I smiled and, before my courage deserted me, turned to join the rest of my intrepid team.

. . .

Armed with rifles, and as many grenades as we could carry, we eased our way as soundlessly as possible to the furthest reaches of the trench. I'd told Thad we would wait ten minutes to allow them to initiate the evacuation process.

I glanced skyward. The sun had disappeared behind a heavy bank of cloud and a fine mist hung over no man's land, drastically reducing visibility. This should work in our favour. The more obscure the divide between the two lines, the longer it would take for the Germans to figure out from which direction we were coming… and, of course, masked the fact there was very few of us.

I studied the fear-riddled faces of my companions.

"Last one home buys a round." I forced a grin, glad to hear a soft chuckle.

"You're on." Bill Marsden, a Grimsby lad, stuck out his hand. We shook.

"Hope you're prepared for a huge tab," Ray Hislop, who hailed from Barnetby, quipped. "I'm gonna need a whisky chaser after this."

"Or two," another chimed in.

Nonsense it might have been, but it steadied us.

The guns fell silent.

Deliberately, I envisaged Eliza. Elfin features, glorious grey eyes, and glossy brown hair curling riotously about her shoulders. The magic of our first kiss, the day we got married, the way she smiled, the bliss of holding her, loving her.

I allowed her image to fill my mind, sent up a heartfelt apology that I was about to break my vow, and surrendered to the inevitable.

"An honour." I dipped my head, and gave the signal.

We ignited and hurled the grenades, willing them to detonate. Crude devices, their effectiveness was debatable and, if handled clumsily, often did more damage to the thrower than the target.

To our relief, each one discharged in a dazzling blast, showering lethal fragments over the enemy. We shimmied up the ladders and, using the explosions as a screen, propelled ourselves over the top as though the hounds of hell were behind rather than in front of us, screaming like banshees.

Ten

July 1915 - Western Front, Flanders
Joe

B lack silence cushioned me. On the periphery of my consciousness, half-formed questions writhed like sycamore keys caught in a gale.

They seemed important.

I tried to squint in my head… a peculiar endeavour… the better to interpret the jumble of words, but the dizzying jig did not abate.

My powers of concentration deserted me, and the seductive song of peaceful oblivion was so inviting.

My slow descent into its cocoon-like comfort was interrupted when I registered something licking at my hand.

What the hell?

Squirming, I tried to flick it away, but it continued.

A shiver of dread ran through me.

Was this how you died? The chill started at your fingertips and slithered through your body until everything keeping you alive was frozen?

Don't be stupid, Joe. I admonished internally. *There's a perfectly logical explanation.*

Where was I? I prised my eyelids apart, to be met by more darkness, simultaneously gaining the impression my body was being gradually crushed under a heavy object.

Flashes of memory pestered. I fought to recall how I had ended up here — wherever *here* happened to be. Something about evacuating the wounded from a series of collapsing trenches.

Images ricocheted around my head but refused to be pinned down. Nothing, except a cacophony of men screaming, and munitions exploding, bodies flying, and the endless eruptions of mud. Thick wet mud.

I *did* recall one of the blokes, who had done some travelling before the war, remarking that the black mud reminded him of a lava flow smothering everything in its path.

You are a repository of useless information, Joe. I would have tutted had I dared open my mouth. As it was, I tried to verify whether I was alive or dead. I could feel the thud of my heart — a good sign. I breathed in fresh air through my nose which was clear of any obstruction and, presumably, the main reason I was not yet dead.

One thing at a time. Can I move my head? A feat I attempted with a modicum of success.

Next — shoulders and arms.

My left arm lay at an awkward angle above my head. This was the one being licked, and the one protecting my nose from the mud. I could move my wrist, but the rest was wedged in position by whatever was on top of me — currently, a welcome immobility.

I flexed my right arm, relieved when pins and needles began radiating up from my fingers, which I clenched into a fist then relaxed, repeating the action until the tingling dissipated.

Blinking, I realised it wasn't dark at all. I was covered by a substantial layer of that bloody mud. I spluttered to spit the foul stuff out of my mouth and, with an effort, wrenched my right arm free.

Immediately, I felt a cool breeze caress my skin, and Eliza's face swam over my vision.

Eliza, oh God, Eliza.

Why was I stuck here, and not back in the trenches, or in a field hospital? There was only one answer… my comrades had not been able to find me. *Was that why I was abandoned and alone under God knows what? Bloody hell, they must think I'd been blown to smithereens by one of those volleys.* My brain careened around the ramifications.

Whatever had been licking my hand transferred its attention to the exposed skin around my eyes. As the mud cleared, I found myself staring up at the biggest dog I'd ever seen.

For one ghastly moment — and given the glut of ghastly moments of late, that in itself was impressive — I contemplated whether there were wolves in Flanders, and this one had found its lunch.

"Help me. Please help me. Someone please get me out from under this mud." My voice sounded muffled and hoarse, but I persevered.

A human face appeared above me.

Willing hands moved whatever held me trapped.

Then the pain started, and so did my screams.

July 1915 - Nettleby-under-Wold
Eliza

Two weeks dragged by, and I still felt as though I was floundering in a quagmire. Everything took twice as long, and my brain refused to function properly. The school told me to take as long as I needed but, in all honesty, I was better working. Time hung too heavily on my hands, and all I could think about was Joe.

There was no body to bury, no gravestone to grieve at, and I was at a loss as to how to deal with his death. I couldn't even cry, despite knowing it might dislodge the hard lump gripping my chest.

Reverend Mitchell, our vicar, suggested I might find solace if I commandeered a small plot at the back of the churchyard as a memorial corner.

It seemed absurd at first, but the more I pondered the idea, the more I liked it. So, with his assistance, I chose a quiet spot at the far side of the graveyard, near the church wall and under a beech tree. Far enough out of the way that I wouldn't disturb anyone whatever time I visited.

The view beyond the church was spectacular and I knew Joe would have enjoyed being laid to rest there.

I went every day. Sitting on the grass under the tree, I told Joe about what we were doing at school, the antics of the children, any village gossip, and how much I loved him.

One morning, I was unnerved to see a huge black dog curled up near the trunk of the old beech, and almost fled.

The creature lifted his head and stared, perceptive amber eyes boring into me, but he didn't move. As his bushy tail thumped the ground rhythmically, he made a curious sound, reminiscent of distant thunder which seemed to echo in the stillness, and closed his eyes.

Cautiously, I approached my usual spot and, trying to ignore the great beast, began my conversation with Joe.

The dog was always there, and I came to find an odd sort of comfort in his presence. I named him Wolf — it was easier than saying 'dog' all the time, and the moniker seemed fitting. Moreover, by giving Wolf a name, I felt closer to Joe, as though this dog was somehow a link between me and the afterlife.

Yes, I realised it was fanciful, but the concept was a balm to my shattered heart, more so than prayer or the solicitude of my friends. I didn't question it.

The weeks crawled by. July became August and, although in my heart I knew I would never recover from the loss of the man I believed was my soulmate, I had to work out how to pick up the pieces of my life.

If not, I feared I might fade away too.

Eleven

July 1915
A farmhouse near the Allied front-line, Flanders
Joe

The next time I opened my eyes, I felt less flattened. It took me a few moments to register I was in a bedroom.

White lace curtains fluttered at the spotlessly clean, open window. The furniture, although sparse, was sturdy. The bed was narrow. I was covered with a colourful quilt, and the pillows were like clouds. It was a long time since I had rested in such luxury.

I tried to sit up, but the movement brought on a wave of pain so acute, I could not prevent the bellow ripped from my lungs.

Footsteps pounded up the stairs towards me. The door flew open, and a woman entered, speaking in gentle tones.

I had absolutely no idea what she was saying but it sounded soothing.

"Je ne comprend pas," I ventured, essaying my limited French, not knowing any Flemish.

"Ah, es tu anglais?"

I forced my brain to work and nodded.

"Yes… err… oui, je suis anglais. Errr… parlez vous anglais?" My words were hesitant, but either I had spoken correctly, or she gathered the gist, because she smiled and patted my arm.

"Un peu."

Between my smattering of French and her — to my embarrassment — much broader grasp of English, we managed to understand each other. I was found under a mutilated horse — *where had the horse come from?* — surrounded by the ravaged remains of several soldiers… whether Allied or German was indecipherable… at the edge of a field the day after an horrendous bombardment.

"We think l'anglais did an attack énorme, because ze Germans 'ave gone… poof." She clapped. "So loud, so much screaming. The errr… hmmm…" She mimed firing a gun. "La fusillade, la cannonade, le coup de feu."

"Gunfire? Shelling?" I made an explosive motion with my hands.

She nodded. "Oui, too much, too much. When it stops, we cannot check, you understand. The danger, he is too close. We wait. One hour, five hours, a night. Then, in the morning, we see no Germans, no Allies, and can look for survivors."

"You risked your lives to save me? Merci beaucoup, merci beaucoup." I was humbled by their courage. This place must be close to the front line.

She gave a fatalistic shrug. "La vie est sacrée. Too many die. Tu es venu défendre cette terre… err… you came to, I think you say, guard our land. So, we guard you." She beamed at me.

"Thank you again." Grateful she had translated, my exhausted brain had given up at life being sacred. She would get no argument from me on that score.

"We thought everyone was dead, but César found you, et voilà, 'ere are you."

"César?" I queried faintly.

"Le chien."

I recalled the huge wolf-like animal towering above my face, making me think I was at death's door, presuming it was Cerberus — Hades' hound. I felt a wry smile tug at my lips, relieved to be wrong.

I ascertained my rescuers had transported me by cart to this farmhouse, barely a mile from the front. I passed out when the horse was hauled off me. Their local doctor diagnosed broken ribs, a smashed ankle, and multiple lacerations.

This was the first time I had regained consciousness since I was discovered and — from the woman's gesticulations — surmised, all were stunned my injuries were not far worse and that I was still alive. Given their lurid descriptions, it seemed I might well owe my life to that damn mud.

"My regiment. They will think I am dead. I must get back to them."

"Tsk, soon. First, rest and heal. I," she pointed to herself, "Adrienne, will 'elp."

The door swung open again. I heard a light footpad but could see no one. A cold nose nuzzled my hand where it lay on top of the covers. A huge head, black fur tipped with tawny, and a tongue lolling from a jaw, which looked capable of tearing off a man's head in one bite, came into view.

"César?" I hazarded, not altogether astutely. Adrienne

nodded. Gingerly, I reached out to stroke the dog's head and fondle his great ears, hearing a deep rumble in response.

"Ahhh, he accepts you. You are now… hmm… les amis… hmmm… the friends."

I stared at the dog whose sharp amber eyes seemed to see right inside me. "Merci beaucoup, César, and again you too, Madame, for rescuing me. I am in your debt."

Adrienne shook her head. "De rien, je vous en prie." Affirming she would return shortly with some food, she left the room, but the dog never moved.

I found myself talking to the creature, more as a distraction from the pain than anything else. How to get a message to my commanding officer before they informed Eliza of my presumed death. How to get to the field hospital, although having seen them, I stood a better chance of survival here.

Tired after even so brief a conversation, I dozed off, my hand resting on César's ruff.

Eliza and I were strolling along to the village. The sun was shining, and the breeze was just enough to keep the heat at bay. We were chattering about this and that, and I couldn't keep my eyes off my wife. Eventually, I could take it no more and, when we reached the fork in the road, I spun her to face me.

"Joe?" She raised a puzzled eyebrow.

"I need to kiss you."

"Well, it would be churlish to stop you." Eliza grinned at me, her beautiful grey eyes, framed by sooty lashes, sparkled with mischief. Her dark hair was already coming undone from the neat twist she had spent ages taming it into, errant strands curling around her lightly tanned, heart-shaped face.

I was endlessly amazed she loved me. I didn't think I was much of a catch. She was a teacher, I a farm labourer, but she stole my heart years ago, the day she smiled at me after taking a tumble, long before I knew what love was. It took me ages to pluck up the courage to court her, little knowing she felt the same way.

I cupped her face, her skin felt like silk against my calloused hands, and I brushed my thumb over her bottom lip.

"I love you, Mrs Elliott."

"I love you too, Mr Elliott. Now stop talking and kiss me."

Our kiss went on and on, passion smouldered and threatened to flare out of control.

Suddenly, she was no longer in my arms. Confused, I looked for her.

Ahead, the sky was black, storm clouds swirled, and Eliza was being sucked away. She screamed my name, but I couldn't reach her, and then she was gone.

"*Eliza!*" I jolted awake, soaked in sweat. My head throbbed, and I ached like the dickens. I sensed movement, then felt cool cloths being applied to my forehead and wrists.

"Hush, mon ami, close your eyes," Adrienne's soft voice entreated. She began to croon a lullaby.

I wanted to fight the lethargy, to stay awake, but sleep won, and I slid back into the darkness.

Twelve

August 1915 - Nettleby-under-Wold
Eliza

I n the days following Joe's... well, I suppose I would have to call it death... I received two letters.

One from Fred Cuthbert, and one from Charlie Townsend — another of Joe's friends.

Their words provided me with a little more detail.

My dear Lizzie,

By now you will have heard from Thad. I do not wish to compound your grief, but I thought it might give you a modicum of comfort to know that Joe died a hero.

Our trenches were collapsing under the constant barrage of artillery, a situation exacerbated by the number of wounded requiring treatment, and heavy rainfall.

To my everlasting shame, it was my idea to create a diversion. All we needed was to get the Hun to fire in another direction, long enough to allow us to pull back to a safer series of trenches.

Thad and his fellow brass, who are all right as officers go, knew it was risky, and our options were growing thinner by the hour. It was a gamble, but we were trapped.

Ideas were pitched and, filtering out the unfeasible, we came up with an almost acceptable plan. Make it look like several sections were going over the top at an unexpected, illogical, and reckless angle, forcing the Germans to re-direct their artillery.

By the time they moved their guns and resumed firing, we had a reasonable chance of getting everyone else to comparative safety. The plan was flimsy at best, but it was all we had.

To my horror, Joe volunteered to lead the charge. I nearly shot him myself, but he would not be swayed.

Lizzie, Joe knew his was, essentially, a suicide mission. He and his mates would be extraordinarily lucky to escape unscathed, but if the few saved the many, he said he could live, he hoped, with that.

We watched them creep towards the end of the ruined trench system, until they disappeared out of our line of sight.

Ten brave men.

My heart was in my mouth and, for the first time in longer than I can remember, I prayed. With every fibre of my being, I prayed they would survive, that Joe would survive.

The firing stopped. There was an uncanny silence, followed by a series of explosions as the grenades detonated.

Then we heard them, screaming blue murder, as they went over the top, heading for the enemy line, guns rattling.

It worked. Lord preserve us, it worked. The Hun scrambled to swivel their weapons, desperate to repel what must have sounded like a horde of Tommys bearing down on them.

Eventually, they got themselves sorted and fired at their new target.

It gave us the window we needed to evacuate the weakened trenches. All the injured were removed to the field hospital and the line held, but none of the ten survived.

Most, we couldn't find. They had vanished without a trace, as completely as though they had never been there. Even those we were able to identify would have died instantly and without pain.

We gained a morsel of satisfaction when we discovered the Germans had suffered grievously under the onslaught, as had their trench, which was duly abandoned.

That probably doesn't help you right now, but maybe in time it will be of some solace.

I am so sorry, Lizzie. I wish it could be different but, as I already said, your Joe was a hero. Without his courage and the bravery of the other nine, we'd all be dead or prisoners.

We all miss him. Joe was well-liked and respected among the lads, and I am honoured to have called him my best friend. My life was better for knowing him.

We are all thinking of you.

Fred.

I set that aside to read Charlie's letter, which mirrored Fred's, except he had described the scene when he risked a quick peek over the top of the trench wall. The image it evoked made me giggle... something I did not think possible.

...even across no man's land I spotted them falling over each other in a blind panic... funniest thing I've seen in a long while.

Mind it was still an eternity, before the buggers managed to manoeuvre their guns to aim at their new target. Oh, begging your pardon at my language, Lizzie.

Honestly, it was farcical and doesn't say much for the calibre of their front-line soldiers...

. . .

Both letters made it clear, the ploy had paid off.

The tragedy being that not one of the ten survived.

Heedless of my dress, I was lying on my stomach under the beech tree in the churchyard, reading the letters out loud to the dog, who watched me through unblinking amber eyes.

"Do you think he suffered, Wolf, or was it instant? I hope it was instant."

Despite the subject of our *conversation*, mirth bubbled up when Wolf cocked his head to one side, for all the world as though contemplating my question. He gave a yip, yawned, stood, turned around, and settled down again in exactly the same spot.

"Am I boring you?" I teased, ruffling his dark fur. He pushed his head into my palm and licked my wrist, a sign he wanted his ears tickling.

"Oh, Joe," I whispered to the sky, giving in to Wolf's insistence. "I wish…" I stopped. *Yes, I wished he was here. I wished he hadn't been killed. I wished our lovemaking the night before he left had created something more tangible than a memory. But he wasn't, he had, and it didn't.*

Images of our life together teased. Our first kiss… the night of the Harvest Dance. It was *the* most wonderful kiss, sending delicious frissons tumbling through me all the way to my toes, I could still recall the heady sensation.

The day he proposed… during one of our strolls. He chose the moment the sun sank below the horizon, to go down on one knee. The fiery beauty of the dusk echoed the sky the evening he asked me to be his girl, the same night we first kissed… so romantic.

I blew a melancholy sigh, eliciting a responding whine from Wolf, who snuggled closer in canine comfort. I rested my head on his and closed my eyes.

Would this pain ever diminish?
Wolf had no answers.

August 1915 - Flanders
Joe

My injuries began to heal. Frustratingly, it was slow going. The Flemish doctor had indicated the damage to my right ankle and foot would likely see me discharged from the army… if I ever got back to camp.

The bones were knitting to his satisfaction, but the nature of the injury had left it misshapen, and I could not, would probably never be able to walk without a stick.

It took time, time I did not have. By now, Lizzie would have been informed of my death. To cause her grief, however inadvertently, was like a bayonet to my heart, and all I wanted was to see her, to prove it was not so.

Adrienne suggested I write, but I explained it would be a waste of their precious paper. When the censors saw a letter from a man declared dead, they would destroy it. I had to get back to my unit.

César was my constant companion while I recuperated. He rarely strayed from the room, even sleeping on the floor next to me.

When nightmares disturbed my rest, he stood by the bed and rubbed his massive head against my arm. Involuntarily, my hand would settle into his fur and, almost immediately, the horror dissipated.

In my less lucid moments, I *did* ponder the possibility, César was possessed of some magical healing power.

As I grew stronger, I told him all about Lizzie. Despite it

being doubtful he understood a word I was blathering — he was Flemish after all — I had the oddest notion he was some kind of subliminal link to my darling wife.

Yes, I know, absurd, but I clung to the belief anyway.

Thirteen

August 1915 – British Army Rest Camp, Flanders
Joe

Bearing my weight on two knotty walking sticks, generously donated by Adrienne, I hobbled up to the officer's tent and rapped on the pole.

The flap was flung open, and a weary-looking Sergeant Major Bernard Williams glared down his hawk nose at me.

He was one of the old school, strict disciplinarian types, but right at that moment I could have hugged him. I managed to restrain myself.

"What?" he barked. It was clear he did not recognise me. Why should he? I was a ghost.

"May I speak with you, or Warrant Officer Jenkins?" I asked politely.

I knew I looked dishevelled. My hair was shaggy and, along with my 'tash, I now sported a beard. My uniform was all but shredded in the blast which had almost killed me, and

I wore a faded cotton shirt under an old pair of Gilles' — Adrienne's husband — work overalls. No wonder Williams could not place me.

"We don't have time for idle chit-chat, man. State your business quickly or leave." He tapped his boot with his stick, one for show rather than necessity.

I heaved myself one step closer.

"Private Joseph Elliott, 5th Lincolnshire Regiment reporting, sir," I said smartly, and saluted.

To his credit, my superior officer managed to retain his composure... by a hair's breadth.

In the shocked silence, I discerned the distant but constant, steady *thunk* of artillery and glanced around. No one else was reacting. Here, behind the lines, the war was nothing more than background noise.

"Elliott?"

I watched as he raked his gaze over my pale and still battered face.

"The devil take me, it *is* you. What... how... where?" He swallowed and gathered himself. "Come in, come in." He lifted the flap and stood aside ushering me in ahead of him. I limped slowly into the dim, stuffy tent, and sank into the closest seat, gratefully.

"Private."

I heard him summon a passing soldier.

"Find Warrant Officer Jenkins and ask him to come here as a matter of urgency. Oh, and organise a brew."

Moments later, the flap opened again, and Thad Jenkins strode in.

Hot on his heels came Jack Phillips bearing a tray. Jack gawked at me, shock written all over his face. How he kept his tongue in check, and the tray level, I have no idea.

Glad to see him in one piece, I tipped him a wink, to be rewarded with a huge grin. He placed the tray on the table and waited to be dismissed, whereupon he shot off, doubtless itching to spread the news.

"What on earth is so important? Has peace been declar...?" Thad started to ask, his tone mocking, only to pause mid-word when he saw me. I could almost hear the the cogs in his brain whirring as he gaped in stupefaction.

"Joe? Good God man, it cannot be. We saw... no... no..." when I made to stand and salute, "...keep your seat." He shook his head and dropped into a chair, absently accepting the tin mug of very strong tea passed to him by Sergeant Major Williams.

I handed Thad the papers from the Flemish doctor, and explained my version of events, which I had pieced together from what little I could recall, along with everything Adrienne and Gilles had told me.

"You must have a guardian angel. Cuthbert and Townsend scoured no man's land for hours with no success... obviously. We found Marsden and Duckworth, well... what was left of them, the rest..." he neither finished his sentence, nor noticed me flinch. Thad wasn't being callous, simply stating the facts.

"We had no alternative but to conclude you had simply disintegrated under the intense shelling. If you had seen the devastation wrought on the remains we did find, you'd understand why this seemed the only plausible explanation. Maybe it will be of some consolation to know, we evacuated everyone safely."

He sucked in a breath. "Joe, telling Eliza was the hardest letter I have ever written. Now, here you are alive." This time, he noticed my expression. "Oh hell, she doesn't know?"

"How could I write to tell her I had survived? The censors would have intercepted and destroyed the letter, concerned it was some weird, coded message from the enemy. How could it be from me? I am officially dead."

Thad nodded in comprehension. He studied the doctor's letter and report thoroughly. "You will have to be examined by our medic, but this looks like grounds for honourable discharge. Along with the others who gave their lives that day, you were recommended to be awarded a posthumous medal for outstanding bravery. This is the first time I have had the joy of being able to amend one of those recommendations to 'survived'." A smile brightened his careworn features.

I grinned at him, suddenly light of heart. "I do not care about the medal. I am just relieved the tactic was not in vain, and the Lincolnshires lived to fight another day."

A busy day of medical checks, filling out paperwork — most of which I would require to prove I was not dead — and catching up with my regiment, ensued. They found me a replacement uniform and boots, and I was treated to a meal, a shave, and a haircut.

By evening I was exhausted, clearly not yet fit, and my ankle was giving me hell. I hunted down Fred, who about burst into tears when he saw me.

"*Joe*! Well, look at you large as life and twice as natural. Thought the lads were pullin' me leg. There was me mourning your death, and you were living in the lap of luxury in a local farmhouse, in a proper bed 'n' all."

"Aye, after being blown up, then buried in the mud under a dead horse, I fancied a little pampering," I parried with a tired wink, then gave him the condensed version of what happened.

"I wrote to Lizzie. I told her what you did for us. Man, you're a hero," he said quietly.

"No, I'm not, Fred. I only did what anyone else would have done in the circumstances." I countered.

He shook his head. "I know creating a diversion was my idea in the first place, but when push came to shove, I don't think I'd have the guts to carry out that particular plan.

"Yes, you would. If you thought it'd save your fellow soldiers, you'd do it in a heartbeat."

"Have you written to Lizzie?" He changed the subject.

"Not yet. They are discharging me, hopefully, I can tell her in person."

"Take a letter to Maisie, would you?"

"Of course." I smiled, and we continued to talk well into the night.

Four days later armed with a pile of letters to distribute around Nettleby-under-Wold, most of Wrawby and half of Brigg, I was boarding a ship bound for Hull.

To my everlasting relief, the sixteen-hour journey was uneventful, and the following morning, we disembarked.

I stood on the dock, breathed in the salty air, and praised the good Lord I was on English soil. My rapidly evaporating patience was tested further when we were escorted to the dispersal centre where *another* day of formalities ensued.

My ankle was throbbing and my head spinning by the time the mountain of forms were completed. How anything got done astounded me.

We were offered train tickets, which were of no use to the handful of us who lived south of the Humber — unless you wanted a long and convoluted journey.

Thankfully, some thoughtful soul arranged transport to the ferry for the first crossing in the morning. It meant an uncomfortable night at the dispersal centre, but none of us was unduly worried.

We were home.

As dawn broke, we boarded the ferry — a curious assortment of passengers from returning soldiers to traders to a flock of goats — chatting with that instant camaraderie typical of people thrown together by chance. Bosom pals for the briefest of interludes — to part, unlikely to meet again.

I leant against the rails watching the sun breach the distant horizon. Colour bled over the landscape and spangles of light danced along the dark river, as though kissing it awake.

Kissing... oh, Eliza... anticipation of a reunion almost stolen from me caused goosebumps and, unobtrusively, I pinched the skin under the cuff of my jacket. *Definitely not dreaming.*

I could not hold back a smile of pure elation.

It was going to be a marvellous day.

When I disembarked, I was fortunate to hitch a ride on a wagon bound for Brigg. The driver, there to collect supplies, agreed to drop me at the crossroads a ten minute walk... or, in my case, perhaps fifteen minute hobble... from my home.

While we trundled along the quiet road, my tension mounted.

Had Lizzie moved on? It was two months to the day since my supposed death. Was someone helping assuage her grief?

In my heart of hearts, I knew it unlikely, but even so far removed from the battlefield, war affected people in unexpected ways.

Fourteen

September 1915 - Nettleby-under-Wold
Eliza

I t was a perfect September day. Not too hot so early in the morning — it was barely half past six — but the colour of the sky told me it would be a scorcher later. A Saturday, I could have slept in, but it was too glorious a day a waste lazing about in bed.

As I cycled through the village, an unusual sensation rippled down my spine... akin to optimism, even happiness.

Perhaps, I was beginning to shed my grief. My mind urging me to take the next step, to embrace the future, whatever it might hold.

The delightful tingles subsided. It was two months to the day since... I let that hang and, instead, concentrated on the balmy breeze lifting my hair, and the familiar fragrance of this mellow land where I had the good fortune to be safe.

Arriving at the churchyard, I parked my bike and hurried to the beech tree.

Wolf was in his customary spot, the dappled light shedding intricate patterns over his inky fur giving him an otherworldly quality.

Smiling at my whimsical notions, I retrieved a brown paper bag full of scraps from my satchel and tipped them out in front of the massive dog, certain he grinned at me while he gobbled the food.

Sitting next to him, I burrowed my hands into his thick ruff, and prattled on to Joe about anything and nothing.

Nettleby-under-Wold
Joe

Beset by unexpected nerves, I knocked on the door. Yes, it was my house, but I had no mind to give Eliza a heart attack by striding in unannounced.

There was no reply.

I waited for a moment then rapped again. Nothing.

Odd, it had only just gone seven thirty and, given it was a Saturday, I was flummoxed by her absence. Weekends were usually the time to enjoy a lie in. I checked the shed; her bicycle was gone.

Frowning, I tried to work out where she could be at this hour.

Maisie! Although I would rather my wife was the first person I saw, I needed Maisie's help, and I could give her Fred's letter at the same time.

. . .

Shortly thereafter, I was standing in the shop wafting a sheaf of papers in front of Maisie's face.

"Joe Elliott, do you *want* to give me apoplexy? You're supposed to be dead."

After apologising profusely, handing Maisie her husband's letter, and promising to share my story later, she deigned to tell me where I would likely find Eliza.

"Only place I can think of is the back of the churchyard. She goes there every day, talks about some great black dog who keeps her company. I think she has too vivid an imagination. I've never seen hide nor hair of such an animal around these parts."

She shrugged. "Mind, whatever it is, even if only in her head, seems to comfort her, so who am I to question it."

Minutes later, I was pushing through the lychgate and limping along the path which led to the back of the churchyard.

As I rounded the last corner, I slowed.

There in front of me was the most beautiful girl in the world.

My Eliza.

Curled up under the beech tree talking to... *wait, was that César?*

I blinked and looked again.

Don't be ridiculous, César is hundreds of miles away in a dusty farmyard in Flanders.

I shook my head.

My heart began to thud. I started forward, and a twig snapped underfoot, the sound echoing in the stillness.

Eliza spun around.

Her jaw dropped. She swayed, her face paled to sheet white, and her eyes widened with shock.

For a split second, I thought she might faint, and hastened across the grass as fast as I could manage, silently cursing my damn ankle.

"*Joe?*" Her strangled sob tore at me.

She scrambled to her feet, as did the dog — who looked so like César, I did another double take.

The creature emitted a deep rumble, exactly as César had done when we first met. The likeness was eerily uncanny.

I seized Eliza's hands, so she knew I was no spirit come to haunt her. She gripped them like a lifeline.

"Are you a ghost?" My wife's voice trembled.

"No, my darling, I am very, *very* real."

"B-but..." A forlorn stutter.

"Eliza. I vowed to come home." I saw her tears brim over, and then she was in my arms. "I will explain later, first things first." I moulded her to me and kissed her with all the pent-up desire I had been forced to quash for what felt like several lifetimes.

I heard her breathing hitch as her arms came around me.

"My Joe," she whispered against my mouth. "You kept your promise."

With a flick of his tail, and unnoticed by either of us, a dark shadow slid silently from the churchyard, with what could only be described as an expression of smug satisfaction curving his massive jowls.

Eliza

The school told me to take a week's holiday — a relief, given I could not focus on anything except Joe.

During the first two days, we never left the house, in fact, we barely left the bedroom. While I cannot deny we indulged in a *lot* of lovemaking, we mostly talked, it was simply more comfortable doing so naked and wrapped around each other.

To be honest, I feared Joe might vanish if I let him go.

He skirted around the day he was injured and the aftermath, telling me stories about life on the front line, of his mates, and how they spent their days.

Making it sound more like an adventure than a battle to the death, he studiously avoided any mention of the grisly truth.

While I lived in a sheltered village far from the trauma of war, I was not naive, and Joe didn't seem to realise the details were blazoned over every newspaper.

It was a deliberate ploy to spare me from the horror and I loved him the more for it. His experiences were harrowing in the extreme but, by the grace of God and the generosity of strangers, he had survived.

I knew it would be some time before Joe was restored to full health, and perhaps one day he might feel able to share the rest. For now, he was safely home — that was all I cared about.

On the third morning, we strolled into the village. Our pace was, by necessity, slow and included frequent interruptions to allow Joe to rest his ankle.

We could take all day. It didn't matter. We had all the time in the world. I managed to quell the shout of unadulterated joy bubbling up inside at that thought.

We took the time to admire the view over the patchwork of farmland and beyond to the wolds.

Harvesting was well underway, neat bales replacing shimmering waves of gold.

Everyone we came across shook his hand, declaring their delight that officialdom, for once, had been mistaken.

We popped into the shop for one or two necessities, where we spent a cheerful half hour with Maisie and Mrs Cuthbert who demanded that Joe tell them *everything*, his news eagerly snapped up by anyone else who overheard.

On the way home, we detoured through the churchyard, to my special place.

There was no sign of Wolf. He had vanished as though he had never been here, and the little corner seemed lonely without his comforting presence.

In tacit agreement, we sank onto the dry grass, enjoying the cool shade of the sprawling beech tree.

"I miss Wolf," I said, unable to keep the sorrow from my voice. "He kept me sane."

We had shared our stories of Wolf and César and, although neither of us would admit it to anyone else, the mystery of their appearance in both of our lives and the solace we gained, was a coincidence we could not ignore, however quixotic.

"For which, I am eternally grateful." Joe pulled me against him, my back to his chest. "I suspect he has gone to comfort some other poor soul and guide them through their grief."

I twisted in his arms to study his face; he was quite serious.

He smiled tenderly and kissed my nose.

"I'm glad we came today," I murmured. "I needed to be certain he wasn't waiting. There's nothing here for me now."

I felt Joe's breath warm against my neck, the beat of his heart against my back.

The same thrill I felt the day he returned simmered through me and, sending up my thousandth prayer of thanks, I added. "Let's go home."

Hand in hand we meandered along quiet pathways, chatting about nothing of any significance — oh, how I loved the mundanity of it.

Reaching our gate, we stopped.

There was a box on the doorstep.

A large box.

It was wobbling.

I glanced up and down the street, there was no one in sight.

I looked at Joe and clutched his fingers a little more tightly.

Extricating his hand from mine, he approached the package with a healthy degree of caution and crouched.

He lifted the lid and a black furry head popped out.

Long, pink tongue lolling from a laughing mouth.

And a pair of the most incredible, ageless amber eyes.

"Wolf!"

"César!"

We spoke in unison, disbelief etched on our faces.

"Well how about that, he's come home," Joe said in far calmer tones than I would have used, and hoisted the wriggling bundle into his arms.

We never discovered who left the box, but Bran, as we named him, became part of our lives so seamlessly it was as though he had always been there... a notion, not without merit.

His presence a subtle reminder to cherish every moment.

The unconditional love of two — *or maybe just one?* — of his kin, our unexpected guardians, meant we could cherish many more.

Fifteen

June 1917 - Nettleby-under-Wold
Lizzie

A plaintive wail cut the stifling warmth of the bedroom, as I flopped back against the pillows, utterly exhausted. For two pins I would take a pair of shears and chop off my hair which was plastered to my head in damp curls.

The cry. *Was everything all right?*

I felt a refreshing waft of air drift through the room as the window was cracked open, and drew a deep breath of the fragrant, early morning summer breeze into my lungs.

A cool cloth was pressed to my hot cheeks, and I tried to gauge the expression on the face hovering above mine.

"Is…?" Words failed me.

"Are you ready to meet your son?" Mrs Merritt, the midwife, asked softly.

"Son...?" I stammered. "W-we have a son?" The fatigue dissipated slightly.

"Aye, and a bonny wee chap he is too." Her gentle Scottish burr washed over me.

"Joe, where's Joe?"

"I'll fetch him, momentarily. First..." Mrs Merritt shoved two extra pillows behind my shoulders and helped me shuffle into a sitting position. She moved to the foot of the bed, murmuring endearments.

I craned my neck but couldn't see. *Oh, do hurry up,* I pleaded, inwardly.

She placed a bundle in my eager arms.

With one finger, I folded back the edge of the blanket and peeked at the tiny face scrunched up in readiness to test the capacity of his lungs.

His eyes opened... blue and, I swore, already wise.

My breath caught.

The most astonishing wave of emotion swept through me, so powerful I might have crumpled to the ground had I been standing. In that split second, I understood what I had dismissed as fanciful.

The lassitude fled.

"Hello, my beautiful boy," I crooned, rocking him. "Welcome to the world."

I was not aware of Mrs Merritt doing what she had to do, my gaze fixed on the scrap of humanity blinking back at me, imprinting his features into my mind.

Mrs Merritt stuck her head out of the door and called for Joe. The thunder of his feet up the stairs, made me grin. In my few moments of lucidity during the last however many hours, I had imagined him pacing around the house, growling at Maisie and Fred who had come to keep him company... and calm — although any chance of the latter would be a fine thing.

"Lizzie?" His question thrown out when he burst in.

"Is fine, laddie. Tired, but a good night's sleep and a few days' rest will put her to rights. I'm away to pop the kettle on." She smiled benignly and vanished.

Joe perched gingerly on the edge of the bed. He stroked my cheek and leant close to kiss me.

"Lizzie," he repeated.

"Joseph Elliott, meet Thomas Frederick Elliott." I passed the baby over, my heart swelling with love as my husband cradled our son, his expression morphing from concerned to awestruck.

"Oh, Lizzie... he is perfect," he husked, and I spotted the suspicion of tears in his eyes.

"Of course," I observed smugly, "he's ours."

Joe smothered a chuckle. "So modest."

"He's part of you and part of me. In my eyes that makes him perfect."

Joe took my hand squeezing gently. "Thank you, Eliza Elliott. I love you."

"Your sentiment, Joseph Elliott is entirely reciprocated." My radiant beam in contrast with my prim reply.

Mrs Merritt bustled in bearing a tray on which stood a pot of tea, a pile of sandwiches, two cups and a glass of what I guessed to be whisky. "Fred reckoned you might need something stronger than tea." She nodded at Joe then at the glass.

"I think Lizzie deserves that more than I." Joe smiled at me.

"Tea will be just fine." I yawned. "That's if I can stay awake long enough to drink it."

"Am I permitted to take Thomas downstairs," Joe ventured… gamely, I thought, given Mrs Merritt's formidable presence. "Maisie and Fred…"

Mrs Merritt's brows knitted, and she looked at me. I did not want Thomas out of my sight, but our friends had been here all night and, although they didn't know it yet, Joe and I wanted them to be godparents. I had no mind to deprive Joe of the joy of introducing them to their godson.

"Don't be long," I tried not to sound clingy. Joe brushed his lips to my forehead.

"I'll be back in a jiffy," he reassured.

"And don't you drop him," Mrs Merritt cautioned, only half in jest, as Joe headed to the door.

"I promise."

"Please thank them for everything," I called after him, oddly bereft.

The door creaked followed by a soft whine, and a cold nose pushed itself into my hand. "Bran." I ruffled the dog's fur. "My precious guardian." I angled my body to drop a kiss on his snout.

"Lizzie, that dog oughtn't be in here," Mrs Merritt sent me a look of reproach.

"Please let him stay, he's been worried," I beseeched.

"Worried, how can a dog be worried, he's a dog," she retorted, although her fierce frown relaxed a trifle.

"He's part of the family too… he was my first baby."

"Eliza Elliott, the things you say. I never did, first baby… heavens to Betsy what will you youngsters come up with next?" she huffed, but her smile told me Bran would not be shooed out.

"Thank you."

"Well, he's not sharing your tea, come on, lovey," Mrs Merritt coaxed me into two sandwiches and half a cup of tea.

Joe came back and, with a grin at the midwife's patently feigned disapproval, settled himself alongside me on the bed. I cast a sleepy eye over my family — my own miracle once thought snatched away was safe and snug.

Supremely content, I yawned again, nestled against Joe, pressed a light kiss on Thomas' head, and drifted off, one hand still buried in Bran's ruff.

The subsequent days vanished in a blur. I had imagined giving birth would be the hardest part but learning the needs of and adjusting to caring for a newborn outweighed that one hundred-fold... and I would not have changed it for the world.

Joe took to being a dad like a duck to water. Nothing fazed him, he was unflappable, even in the face of my minor panics... of which there were *many*.

Every day when he got home, didn't matter how late or how tired he was, he bundled Thomas into the pram and, with Bran at his side, walked into the village, giving me chance to rest.

He mollified my concerns about his ankle, arguing that the exercise helped strengthen the damaged joint. I think he simply relished those moments with his son, moments repeated when Rose and then Arthur were born.

On November 11th, 1918, peace was declared, and the world took stock. Such a catastrophe must never happen again. The casualties had been astronomical, numbers I could scarcely comprehend, and it had laid waste to half of Europe.

. . .

In our quiet corner of England, life resumed its gentle rhythm, tranquillity slowly supplanted turmoil, and our faith in humanity was renewed.

Long may it reign.

Epilogue

September 1939 – Nettleby-under-Wold
Eliza

In absolute silence, six friends gathered around the wireless to hear Mr Chamberlain announce we were at war with Germany.

We stared at each other in stunned disbelief.

Two decades ago, the world's rulers had agreed the Great War... and there was *nothing* great about it... was the war to *end* all wars. How could they go from 'it must never happen again,' to this?

I thought about those restless souls haunting the battle-fields who had fought and died to ensure an everlasting peace, of the innumerable casualties — so many of whom were unable to escape the after-effects. It appeared their sacrifice was in vain.

I could not fathom the evil which had perpetrated this atrocity. My incredulity exacerbated by the knowledge that this time our children would be called up to fight… *our children.* Ice formed around my heart, and I closed my eyes, trying to stem the dread roiling through me.

Attuned to my every emotion, Joe draped an arm around my shoulders and drew me against him. I looked him in the eye. "We need another miracle," my voice cracked.

"We'll pray for one," he whispered in my ear and kissed my temple.

November 1939 – Brigg Station
Joe

A bright autumnal morn saw us huddled near the clock on the platform at Brigg Station. The wind was blustery, and clouds scudded overhead, but there was enough warmth in the weak sun to banish the worst of the cold.

All around, we could hear the overly cheerful chatter of people determined not to let emotions undermine composure.

Our little group was unusually quiet. The things we needed to say had already been said; to reiterate them would reduce every last one of us to tears.

Unable to countenance a public farewell, Rose and Arthur said their goodbyes at home, as had Maisie and Fred's other children.

The train chugged to a halt. Passengers spilled out onto the crowded concourse, mingling with those trying to board.

On any other day, the chaotic scene would have been comical.

Not today.

Too soon the hordes dissipated. My stomach knotted.

"We'll see you soon, Thomas." I was impressed by Lizzie's stoic façade as I enfolded the three of us into a family hug. "I love you... and please watch out for Hope," she entreated, rubbing the smear of lipstick off our son's cheek.

"As long as I'm able... you know Hope doesn't like being managed." Thomas grinned and kissed his mother.

"Dad." He shook my hand. I gripped it hard, committing his features to memory... as though that was in any way necessary, unable to credit this tall, handsome young man, heading off to war was the same child I had rocked to sleep in my arms. Where did the years go?

Now the moment had arrived. I wanted to stop time, grimly aware of the nightmare awaiting him. I drew him close. "I love you, son."

"You too, Dad. Look after Mum," he muttered and was on the train before I could answer.

The guard blew his whistle, and, in the blink of an eye, the platform emptied, save four people.

With a long hoot and a billow of steam, the train began to move.

Lizzie's calm shattered.

I mouthed a goodbye to Fred and Maisie who were standing under the clock, and ushered my sobbing wife out of the station, biting my own lips to stem unmanly tears.

That night, wrapped up warmly to stave off the frosty air, Lizzie and I — as was our habit, hot mug of tea in hand and Titus, a descendent of Bran, sprawled at our feet — sat on the front step to admire the stars. They looked slightly veiled… a harbinger? Conceivably, given the mushrooming global catastrophe.

All was quiet.

Titus lifted his great head and bayed, the eerie howl rolling back to us in soft echoes as the other dogs in the vicinity joined in the canine chorus.

Memories of Wolf and César reared up in my head. Before I could stop myself, I slid my free hand under the dog's chin and stared into his shrewd amber eyes.

"Guard them well."

I swear he nodded.

Author's Note

My great grandfather, Joseph Elliott, was killed on 4th July 1915 in Flanders.

A member of the 5th Battalion Lincolnshire Regiment, he was 36 years old when war broke out, had already served in the Boer War, and had no need to re-enlist.

He, like so many others, answered the call to protect King and Country. He, like so many others sacrificed his life in the commission of that duty.

He is one of 669 soldiers buried in the Brandhoek Military Cemetery in Ypres, Belgium.

I have read copies of letters sent to his widow from his comrades, who made it clear Joe was well-liked and respected.

A snapshot into the life of a man I never met, touched my heart, and I wanted to give him, albeit posthumously, a happy ending.

Originally published in an anthology, I have revised and extended what had been a short story to create this novella, the first in a trilogy set in rural Lincolnshire against the backdrop of the First World War.

Nettleby-Under-Wold is a fictitious village, as are all the characters, except Joseph and Eliza Elliott, but several places referred to in the series can be found on a map, most of which are where I spent many happy hours while growing up.

The 5th Battalion Lincolnshire Regiment was a successor to an infantry unit originally raised in 1685 as The Earl of Bath's Regiment of Foot during the Monmouth Rebellion.

Eventually it became the 10th (North Lincolnshire) Regiment of Foot, and then simply the Lincolnshire Regiment.

Whatever its title, the regiment has served in numerous British Army campaigns throughout its existence and continues today under the umbrella of The Royal Anglian Regiment.

The sphinx on the badge (and used as an ornamental break in all three books) was granted by Royal Approbation for the regiment's service in the campaign against Napoleon in Egypt.

As far I can determine, the badge is still displayed on the Colours and uniforms of the successors of the Lincolnshire Regiment.

Yes, I am a very proud Great Granddaughter.

Joseph... this is an homage to your courage, to the lads of the Lincolnshire Regiment, and to all who serve their country in what ever capacity.

NB: While the part played by the 5th Lincolnshires in WW1 is well documented and the campaigns they were involved in form the basis of each story, these three novellas are a work of fiction, and I used artistic licence to weave certain scenarios.

About the Author

Rosie Chapel lives in Perth, Australia with her hubby and three furkids. When not writing, she loves catching up with friends, burying herself in a book (or three), discovering the wonders of Western Australia, or — and the best — a quiet evening at home with her husband, enjoying a glass of wine and a movie.

Website: www.rosiechapel.com

Other Books by Rosie Chapel

The Unconventional Duchess

Rescuing Her Knight

Elusive Hearts - *An Unexpected Romance*: Book One

His Fiery Hoyden

A Regency Duet

A Regency Christmas Double

Fate is Curious

A Christmas Prayer *with Ashlee Shades*

The Lady's Wager

Winning Emma

A Love Impossible

Unravelling Roana

Love Kindled

Fairy Tale Romance

Chasing Bluebells

Contemporary Romances

Of Ruins and Romance

All At Once It's You

Cobweb Dreams

Just One Step

His Heart's Second Sigh

Dystopian Romance

Echoes & Illusions *with Rori Bleu*

Historical Fiction/Romance

The Pomegranate Tree

Hannah's Heirloom - Book One

Hoping to trace the origins of an ancient ruby clasp, a gift from her long dead grandmother, Hannah Wilson travels to the fortress of Masada with her best friend, Max. Strange dreams concerning a rebel ambush begin to haunt Hannah and following a tragic accident, she slips into the world of Ancient Masada.

A woman out of time, Hannah must rely on her instincts and her knowledge of what will befall this citadel to survive. Will she escape, or is she doomed to die along with hundreds of others as Masada falls — and what does any of this have to do with an ancient ruby clasp?

Echoes of Stone and Fire

Hannah's Heirloom - Book Two

Pompeii - a vibrant city lost in time following the AD79 eruption of Vesuvius. Now rediscovered, archaeologists yearn for an opportunity to uncover the town's past. Some things, however, are best left alone - revealing the secrets hidden beneath the stones could prove perilous. Hannah and Max are brought to Pompeii by a surprise invitation to join an excavation team who are trying to uncover the city's long history.

After entering an excavated house that bears a Hebrew inscription, Hannah's two worlds collide, and she falls back through time to ancient Pompeii. A place where her ancestor is a physician to gladiators engaged in mortal combat, where riotous mobs run amok and where a ghost from the past returns to haunt her.

Will Hannah and her loved ones manage to escape the devastation she knows is coming, before the town is engulfed in volcanic ash? Will she ever find her way back to Max the love of her life, waiting not so patiently millennia away? Or will echoes be all that remain?

Embers of Destiny

Hannah's Heirloom - Book Three

AD80 - Hannah and Maxentius must embark on a new journey to Northern Britannia. This harsh frontier is far from the comforts of Rome and danger lurks where least expected; a garrison of soldiers, some unhappy with their isolated posting; local tribes, outwardly accepting of their Roman occupier, but who may still resent the seizure of their lands.

Millennia away, Hannah Vallier finds a familiar item while working in a museum near Hadrian's Wall. It is the pomegranate; carved by Maxentius on Masada. Before Hannah can discuss it with Max, disaster strikes! Believing her husband has been killed, Hannah retreats into the past, her soul melding with that of her ancestor, but with little idea of what they could face. Is the risk from the conquered tribes, or much closer to home?

As rebellion threatens to shatter a fragile peace, Hannah's heart whispers that just maybe Max isn't dead and that he is calling her home. Can she trust her heart, or will she remain caught out of time, her destiny floating away like embers on a breeze?

Etched in Starlight

Hannah's Heirloom - Prequel

Maxentius - a Roman soldier fresh from the battlefields of Armenia, arrives to take command of the military outpost of Masada, Herod's isolated citadel in the Judaean desert. A seemingly mundane posting after years of warfare, Maxentius finds it more challenging to maintain a focused garrison than to face the wrath of the Parthians across a disputed frontier.

Hannah - a young Hebrew physician spends her days dealing with injuries from street brawls, deprivation, disease and loss. As her beloved Jerusalem plunges into chaos, her brother — who belongs to a band of rebels determined to drive out their Roman occupiers — tells her of their plans to storm a desert fortress and steal the weapons stored there, persuading his reluctant sister to go with him.

Masada - following the ambush, Hannah finds and treats three badly wounded Roman soldiers. In the aftermath and against impossible odds, Hannah and Maxentius realise that they are more than healer and captive, their fate already etched in starlight.

Prelude to Fate

For Lucia, staring into the jaws of an horrific death, escape seems impossible.

Rufius Atellus, a veteran Roman soldier, is appalled when he recognises one of the victims about to be executed. Surely this is a ghastly mistake?

A ferocious she-wolf, anticipating a tasty meal, suddenly finds herself under a human's control.

In an unexpected twist, and as danger threatens, the lives of all three become inextricably entwined.

Was it chance brought them together in that theatre of bloodshed, or simply a prelude to fate?

Legacy of Flame and Ash

A Hannah's Heirloom Story

An unremarkable family ring — lost when its owner was killed in the catastrophic eruption of Vesuvius — is excavated after nearly two millennia buried under tons of pumice and ash, setting off an extraordinary sequence of events.

A brazen robbery, and the ring is lost again. The theft and subsequent investigation, inspire twelve-year-old Cristiano Rossi to dedicate his life to the search and recovery of stolen artefacts.

Fast forward twenty years. Whispers of a rare item being offered for sale on the black market, initiates a joint operation between the Italian and British branches of the, colloquially named, Art Squad.

Hannah Vallier and her tech savvy assistant, Bryony Emerson — whose abilities to track down the untraceable, led to them assisting the UK Art and Antiquities Unit — have unearthed an intriguing thread. Reluctantly, Cristiano agrees to team up with the pair to thwart the traffickers, retrieve the artefact and, hopefully, dismantle the site.

What ought to be a routine assignment is complicated by a rogue operative, an unexpected romance, an ancient connection, and a *very* angry ghost!

A Guardian Unexpected

The Nettleby Trilogy: Book One

August 1914: Europe is on the brink of catastrophe. In a small village in rural Lincolnshire, a wife kisses her husband goodbye.

Childhood sweethearts, Eliza and Joe have only been married two years. They could not have imagined how soon they would be torn apart by war, nor that the most unexpected of guardians would offer them hope during their darkest hours.

Under the Clock

The Nettleby Trilogy: Book Two

England 1908: Under the clock, on a sleepy station platform nestled in rural Lincolnshire, an unexpected romance blossoms.

Maisie: Every Friday, at precisely five to six, a handsome young man arrives at the station. I know the time because I can see the clock.

The train pulls in, punctual as always, and among the alighting passengers is an elderly gentleman. The young man greets him with a smile and a handshake, then tucks his arm through the older man's and they leave the platform.

Every Friday.

Occasionally, we exchange a glance or two and, to be fair, I suspect I notice him more than he notices me.

Fred: I count the hours until Friday afternoon comes around. Not only because this marks the start of the weekend but also, and more importantly, I get to see the flower girl. I am clueless as to her name, yet my heart begins to race the minute the station comes into view. I almost run up the steps onto the platform, hoping for a glimpse of her bright smile.

Every Friday.

I doubt she ever notices me. I'm just a village lad, one more faceless person in the throng.

Then again, you never know what might happen… in an innocuous corner of a quiet platform…

…under the clock

Evie's War

with Rori Bleu

World War II catapulted ordinary people into extraordinary service to save the world from an insidious evil... even if that meant being forced to do things which, under normal circumstances, would be considered abhorrent.

Genevieve Rousseau, Evie to a select few, was one such person who could not escape this fate. Despite her covert endeavours to liberate Paris from the Germans, she finds herself labelled a collaborator and an enemy of the French Republic.

Her only hope of vindication lies in helping a dangerously handsome American, with questionable motives, to uncover the Germans' final revenge.

Could struggling to resist Major Jack Donovon prove to be the decisive battle in Evie's War?

Regency Romance

Once Upon An Earl

Linen and Lace - Book One

When Fate saw fit to intervene in the life of Giles Trevallier, the very respectable Earl of Winchester, by dropping a female — soaked to the skin and with no memory of who she is or how she came to be there — literally at his feet, no one could have predicted the outcome.

While uncovering her identity, Giles realises he is falling hopelessly in love with his mystery guest, who unbeknownst to him, is succumbing to similar emotions; but, when the heart is involved, a thoughtless word or gesture can thwart even Fate's best-laid plans.

Faced with misunderstandings, whispers of scandal, secret documents and foreign agents, their chance at a happy ever after seems elusive, but fairy tales often happen when least expected, and love — however inconvenient — usually finds a way to conquer all.

To Unlock Her Heart

Linen and Lace - Book Two

Abused by a duke, and shunned by Society, relief seems at hand when Grace Aldeburgh is bequeathed a house in a small village, far from malicious gossips.

Once there, a tentative friendship blooms between Grace and Theo Elliott, the local doctor, who has already resolved to be the man to unlock her heart.

Just when happiness appears to be within her grasp, her erstwhile tormentor once again stalks Grace. After a failed kidnap attempt, the duke's quest culminates in an acrimonious confrontation, and the reason for his venal pursuit becomes agonisingly clear.

NB: This book contains adult themes and situations which, although minimal might be a trigger for some.

Love on a Winter's Tide

Linen and Lace - Book Three

Every day, Helena disappears into a world few acknowledge, helping the poor, downtrodden, and abused. A husband is the last thing she can be bothered with.

Busy managing his shipping line, Hugh Drummond sees no need for a wife, whose only joy is dancing and frivolity. If — and it was a huge if — he ever married, it would be to a woman as capable as he, not some giddy society Miss.

Then, Hugh meets Helena and despite their resolve, fate, it seems, has other ideas. As their attraction deepens however, treachery threatens to tear them apart. Will they uncover the perpetrator in time, or will their love be swept away, lost forever on a winter's tide?

A Love Unquenchable

Linen and Lace - Book Four

Jessica Drummond, a bright and cheerful young woman, rarely gives romance, let alone love, a thought. Long hours working in her brother's shipping office affords little chance of her ever meeting an eligible bachelor.

Duncan Barrington, veteran of the Napoleonic Wars, believes himself wounded in both body and soul. He has no intention of inflicting his demons on anyone, certainly not a beautiful and, in his opinion, irresponsible city lady.

One cold and snowy morning, the plight of a bedraggled puppy throws Jessica and Duncan together and, as a spark of something indefinable yet wholly unquenchable begins to burn, it is unclear who rescued whom.

A Hidden Rose

Linen and Lace - Book Five

After witnessing his mother's grief at the loss of his father, Nick Drummond resolved never to cause someone he loved such distress. Even the happiness of his siblings would not sway him — until he met Rose.

Rose Archer was almost content assisting her doctor father in a tiny fishing village in the north of Yorkshire. To experience the world beyond, a tantalising dream — until she met Nick.

Unexpectedly, the impossible becomes possible, and the renounced — desired above all things, but the shipwreck that brought them together, may yet tear them apart. Will Nick learn to trust his heart, or will his love for Rose remain forever hidden

The Daffodil Garden

Horrifically scarred during the war, William Harcourt - Marquis of Blackthorne - prefers to spend his days in the quiet of his daffodil garden; plants do not pity, turn away, or judge.

Lucy Truscott, whose life is far removed from that of the *ton*, has no idea that by saving the life of a young woman, to whom she bears an uncanny resemblance, her own will be placed in mortal danger.

A chance encounter leads to something more. William begins to trust that Lucy sees the man beneath the scars, while Lucy is persuaded that love might actually transcend status.

Unfortunately, before their courtship has really begun, someone has every intention of ending it - permanently.

The Unconventional Duchess

Refusing to suffer the humiliation of her husband flaunting his mistress at Society events, the newly married Duchess of Wallingstead, Ella Lennox, takes control of her life. She leaves London for the family's country seat in remote Yorkshire.

A woman alone, Ella spends the next four years turning a cold, grim house into a home, and transforming the fortunes of the estate. Not afraid of hard work, she soon earns the respect of those around her with her determination and unconventional attitude.

Out of the blue, the duke arrives. Resigned to another arduous visit, Ella is stunned when it seems he is attempting to court her.

Impossible!

Could her dream of a happy marriage be about to come true?

Everything hangs on a snowstorm, a herd of cows and an uninvited guest!

Rescuing Her Knight

The *de Wiltons* — Book One

A story, invented to keep a little girl distracted, marks the beginning of another tale. One destined to remain unfinished for twenty years.

At thirteen, Adam Marchmain became Kitty de Wilton's 'Knight of the Garden' — a title bestowed following an accident which resulted in six-year-old Kitty having her knee sutured. Kitty never forgot his gallantry, but pledges made as children rarely survive into adulthood.

Their paths separated until Fate decreed, they meet again.

Widowed, badly disfigured and his sight ruined, Adam returns to his family home, a shadow of his former self.

Similarly afflicted, although her scars are invisible, Kitty — against her better judgement — is persuaded to help Adam banish his demons. This requires a subterfuge which, if discovered, might shatter more than the bonds of friendship forged two decades previously.

To Kitty, determined to break through the shield Adam has erected, the risk is worth it.

To see his smile and hear his laughter.

To rescue the knight of her childhood.

Just when a fairy tale ending is within her grasp, Kitty is threatened by the man who murdered her husband. In a cruel twist the tables are turned, and Kitty is the one who needs rescuing.

Elusive Hearts

An Unexpected Romance — Book One

What happens when two people whose elusive hearts fight an indefinable attraction, neither looked for nor desired, dare to dream?

When her fiancé and sister abscond to Gretna Green on her wedding day, Sapphira Beresford longs to escape, to avoid the gossipmongers gloating over her misfortune. Disillusioned, she is determined not to be burnt again, swearing off romance and marriage.

A fortuitous invitation sees her embarking on a journey to Pompeii where she meets Leofwin Colleville, reclusive marquis, amateur antiquarian, and her host for the duration.

Although enamoured of the ruins gradually being unearthed and ecstatic to have the opportunity to assist, Sapphira is troubled by her host's attitude, which blows hot and cold.

A confirmed bachelor, Leofwin Colleville is happiest surrounded by ancient ruins, and would prefer to brave the whole of Napoleon's armies alone, than face a lady on the hunt for a husband. The arrival of an unexpected guest throws his unencumbered existence into turmoil, but the harder he strives to maintain his distance, the more she gets under his skin.

Sparks fly and, as Leofwin's truculence undermines Sapphira's already battered confidence, her adventure of a lifetime seems doomed to disaster.

Until the day she runs afoul of greedy treasure hunters.

In the aftermath what was scorned becomes the one thing they crave above all else, but when it comes to the heart, nothing is ever simple.

His Fiery Hoyden

A Novella

Livvy has no respect for the nobility; they let her down when she most needed them. Why should she accede to their demands now?

Philip, Lord Harrington, is stunned to discover the young heir to the dukedom lives a stone's throw away in a ramshackle cottage, and resolves to restore the child to his birthright.

They meet in a clash of wills, but just when it seems Livvy might surrender, the victory Philip desires, may not taste all that sweet.

A Regency Duet

Luck be a Pirate

Luck wasn't something retired pirate Kennet Alexson believed in — good or bad. However, even he had to concede that landing a job at Trentams shipyard, and meeting Lynette Collins, was more than coincidence.

Fortune it seemed, was smiling on him for once.

As Kennet adjusts to life on dry land, his friendship with Lynette deepens into something far more enduring, and what once seemed elusive now becomes possible.

Unfortunately, fate has other plans, and Kennet's good luck is about to run out.

The Highwayman's Kiss

Surrendered Hearts — Book One

Nothing exciting had ever happened to Juliette St Clair. Her days were spent assisting her father or calling on friends, wandering art galleries, taking constitutionals or, and more preferably, escaping into her books. Her evenings her evenings — an endless round of balls, where she preferred to remain invisible.

Until the day she was robbed by a highwayman.

A Regency Christmas Double

Heart Rescued

Four years since Jasper lost the woman he was hoping to marry. Four years since he closed his heart and withdrew from Society. He has no idea his reclusive existence is about to be shattered.

Enter his sister's best friend, Harriet, a flame haired beauty, who needs his help.

Reluctantly he agrees and as they spend time together, it is clear their feelings run deep. Although Harriet affects Jasper in a way no woman ever has, he believes her to be out of his league ~ but it's Christmas and she might just be the one to melt his frozen heart

Catch a Snowflake

Romance often blossoms in the most unlikely of places - but in a ward full of wounded soldiers - surely not?

When Lucas Withers comes face to face with Jemima Parsons - a young woman who blames him for her brother's injury - falling in love is the last thing on their minds. What neither of them anticipated, was the magic of snowflakes.

Fate is Curious

A Novella

Happily, ever after? No such thing! Bereft, following her beloved husband's sudden death, Lady Charlotte Sherbrooke has lost her belief in romantic nonsense.

Successful shipping merchant, Zacharie Romain, is no stranger to loss; his business can be hazardous. Moreover, his wife died in childbirth and even though it happened a decade ago, he has no mind to expose himself to such sorrow again.

They meet in less than joyful circumstances but, as the year turns and grief diminishes, the woes of a small boy become the catalyst for something wholly unexpected. Can Charlotte and Zacharie trust what Fate has in store or will past heartbreak prevent them from taking a chance on love?

A Christmas Prayer

with Ashlee Shades

A Short Story

An entreaty from a frightened child.

Orphaned and only nine, Caroline Thorne has to grow up before her time. She is doing everything she can to keep what is left of her family together and out of the workhouse but is terrified her prayers are not being heard. Or maybe they are...

A petition from a woman desperate for a family.

A chance meeting with three orphaned siblings, tugs at Elizabeth Barrington's heart strings. Thus far, she and her husband have not been blessed with children and, as Christmas approaches, a plan begins to form - one which might just be the answer to her prayers.

Two Christmas prayers, as different as they are the same.

Will they hear and, more importantly, heed the answer?

The Lady's Wager

Surrendered Hearts- Book Two

A Novelette

Ged Mowbray will do anything to avoid being married off to the suitable prospects his parents insist on parading in front of him.

Melissa Bouchard is under no illusion her sizeable dowry is the attraction to suitors, not her.

An overheard conversation leads to an offer too good to refuse, but what happens when a lady's wager, becomes a gamble on the happily ever after, you did not even realise you wanted?

Winning Emma

Surrendered Hearts - Book Three

A Novelette

Randolph Craythorpe — earl, covert operative, and occasional highwayman — believed his dalliance with Lady Felicity Hartwich would lead to marriage. It did, but not to him! The arrival of an unwelcome guest, however, provides the perfect opportunity to indulge in a little retaliation.

Emma Newbury accompanies her cousin, Lady Charity Anscombe, to London for the Christmas season. Once there, she comes face to face with the three men who witnessed the humiliating aftermath of her father's disgrace — one of whom, to her irritation, has taken up residence in her dreams.

Their infrequent encounters only serve to confuse but, while winter tightens its grip on the city, what was inconceivable becomes the one thing for which they both yearn, yet bound by Society's rules, cannot admit.

As the snow falls, Randolph begins to understand that to win Emma, he will have to surrender.

A Love Impossible

A Regency M/M Novelette

Tasked with investigating a heinous crime, Edward Lindsay travels from London to Dublin — a city which holds too many memories — in the guise of guardian to his sister. He knew it could be hazardous, and relished the challenge, but that wasn't what caused his stomach to tighten as they approached landfall.

Dublin held more than just a murderer.

There was also Aidan.

While attending a party, Aidan Griffen is astonished when he comes face to face with a man who fled Dublin two years previously. A man he has desperately tried to forget.

As Edward closes in on his quarry, a fire, deliberately extinguished, is rekindled. But what of it? Edward and Aidan share a love impossible, and to acknowledge their feelings — more dangerous than confronting a killer.

Is there any hope of a happily ever after?

Unravelling Roana

A Regency Novelette

Tired of being ignored by her husband, Roana Dumont, Countess of Brooketon does the one thing guaranteed to get his attention. She runs away… to Venice, leaving behind a set of riddles for him to solve… *if* he feels their marriage is worth saving.

Gideon Dumont, 6th Earl of Brooketon is flabbergasted when he discovers his wife has apparently vanished off the face of the earth. A series of puzzles, the only clue as to her whereabouts.

The question is… will he unravel them?

Love Kindled

A Regency Novelette

Recently widowed, Amelia Ingram - Countess of Gresham, decides to shake off the fetters from her arranged and loveless marriage. Exploiting her new-found independence, Amelia indulges her yearning to explore - incognito.

Her ploy works so well, she receives an offer of employment from the dangerously handsome, Rupert Latimer - Earl of Badlesmere. On impulse, she accepts and finds herself governess to Cate, a delightful scamp of a child. What began as a bit of a game on Amelia's part, evolves into something far more profound, and a flame she presumed impossible to ignite, is kindled.

An unexpected turn of events leads to yet another offer. This time there is far more at stake and, determined history not repeat itself, Amelia confesses her ruse.

Rupert has been burnt once. Will he douse the spark, or take a risk and trust his heart?

Fairy Tale Romance

Chasing Bluebells

A Fairy Tale Novella

Once upon a time, somewhere in France, there was a man whose reckless obsession led him down a dark path — one which, ultimately, cost him his life.

That ought to have been the end of it.

Regrettably, as is so often the case, those who least deserve it, suffer for the actions of others.

A decade after being sent away, Sebastien Daviau returns to the little village where everything began. Hoping to lay the ghosts of his childhood to rest, he studiously ignores the possibility, he might run into Charlotte de Montbeliard.

As luck would have it, Charlotte is the one who runs into him… well, his horse… and although the brief encounter leaves a lasting impression, neither recognises the other.

A name revealed causes a freak accident, catapulting Sebastien's past into his present, and bringing him face to face with a man whose reputation would intimidate the most ardent of suitors.

Can whatever is blossoming between Charlotte and Sebastien survive the challenge imposed, or is their happily ever after about to fade as quickly as the bluebells they loved to chase?

Contemporary Romance

Of Ruins and Romance

Kassandra Winters has intrigued Gabriel St Germain since he accidentally knocked her flying outside her university professor's office. Her face haunts his dreams, yet he never expected to see her again. So, he is surprised when she appears, as though destined to do so, in the middle of a ruin, and he concocts a plan to win her heart.

Gabriel's old-fashioned courtship touches something deep inside Kassie and, although struggling to believe someone as handsome as Gabriel could possibly be interested in her, she soon realises she has fallen irrevocably in love with him. However, just as Kassie shares everything of herself with Gabriel, her world comes crashing down.

Can their romance survive, or will it fall in ruins, like the relics of antiquity that brought them together?

All At Once It's You

When Alex arrives in the small village of Rosedale Abbey, to take up a position as a research assistant for a renowned archaeologist, the last thing she is looking for, or expects to find, is love.

Jake was perfectly happy with the status quo. When it came to relationships, he didn't do committed or long term. He called the shots, and if his current flame didn't like it, she knew what to do. A philosophy, which served him well - until he met Alex.

Romance blooms, but even as the untamed wilderness of the North Yorkshire moors weaves its spell, a long-buried secret might yet jeopardise their happily ever after.

Cobweb Dreams

A Novella

A holiday on the Scottish isle of Mull was just the break Chloe Shepherd needed, an escape from her boring office job and her complete lack of anything resembling a social life. Romance, it seems, isn't on the cards and, although Chloe dreams of finding her soulmate she is beginning to believe love is like cobwebs — spun overnight, only to vanish in the early morning breeze.

Under sufferance, Dominic Winters makes a flying visit to Mull to check on a rental property owned by his family. He hasn't got time for this — so indulging in a holiday fling is the last thing on his mind.

A lamb stuck in a bog proves a most unexpected matchmaker and, while Mull weaves its magic, Chloe wonders whether those fragile cobwebs might be far more stubborn than she thought.

Just One Step

A Short Story

In the aftermath of an horrific car accident, Daisy Forrester travels to Italy - hoping, so far from her memories, she might begin to heal.

Archaeologist, and single father, Adam Willoughby is too busy looking after his young daughter to give romance let alone love, a thought.

Neither expects a chance encounter in an ancient ruin to be anything more, but sometimes, that's all it takes.

His Heart's Second Sigh

A Novella

Reuben Faulkner and Paige Latimer are two happily single people, who have no desire to upset the status quo.

Unexpectedly, they are thrown together, only to discover both want far more than a casual friendship.

Just when things take an interesting turn, Reuben's past catches up with them, and threatens to derail their blossoming romance before it has chance to start.

Dystopian Romance

Echoes & Illusions

The Hunters - Book 1

Twenty years after a global plague, the remnants of civilisation struggle to eke out an existence in a world where humanity is secondary to survival.

On the outskirts of a once vibrant Rome, Gabriel tends his vineyard. From dawn to dusk, he strives to carve out a living, while caring for Bianca, his heavily pregnant wife.

Life might be tough, but at least he had an income, meagre though it was. Trouble seemed a distant memory, until the day he notices their neighbours are not at work in the adjacent fields.

A gruesome discovery sparks a chain of events to rival the conflicts Rome witnessed at the height of its power. Gabriel and Bianca must pit their wits and their lives against a formidable opponent, in an attempt prevent an atrocity none could have predicted.

A bond, forged in a snowy field and strengthened in a city under siege, is put to the ultimate test.

In a world of echoes and illusions, is their love strong enough to surmount the odds, or will it crumble to dust like the empire their enemies are striving to replicate?